MAGIC
AND
MAYHEM

ARCANE SOULS WORLD: THE WRONG WITCH BOOK 2

ANNIE ANDERSON

MAGIC & MAYHEM
ARCANE SOULS WORLD
The Wrong Witch Book 2

International Bestselling Author
Annie Anderson

Edited by Angela Sanders
Cover Design by Tattered Quill Designs

www.annieande.com

BOOKS BY ANNIE ANDERSON

THE ARCANE SOULS WORLD

GRAVE TALKER SERIES

Dead to Me

Dead & Gone

Dead Calm

Dead Shift

Dead Ahead

Dead Wrong

Dead & Buried

SOUL READER SERIES

Night Watch

Death Watch

Grave Watch

THE WRONG WITCH SERIES

Spells & Slip-ups

Magic & Mayhem

Errors & Exorcisms

THE ETHEREAL WORLD

PHOENIX RISING SERIES

(Formerly the Ashes to Ashes Series)

Flame Kissed

Death Kissed

Fate Kissed

Shade Kissed

Sight Kissed

ROGUE ETHEREAL SERIES

Woman of Blood & Bone

Daughter of Souls & Silence

Lady of Madness & Moonlight

Sister of Embers & Echoes

Priestess of Storms & Stone

Queen of Fate & Fire

For my readers. Thanks for the wild ride.

Everyone is a moon and has a dark side which he never shows to anybody.

— MARK TWAIN

CHAPTER ONE

WREN

I was married to a werewolf.

Funny, I didn't recall saying "I do" anywhere in the last week, but there I was sitting on the tattered couch in Nico's cabin beneath a mound of blankets. A heating pad had been put under my back to combat the touch of cold I still had after tromping all over a mountain barefoot in a snowstorm, and while the apple cider someone had scrounged up was awesome, I was trying not to barf it all over the rough planked floor.

Concussions were a bitch.

All the while, I watched my wolfy husband and his boss square up against my grandmother.

Fun times.

And it wasn't like I could say anything about it right then—not with Eloise Bannister staring down at me with wrath in her eyes.

My grandmother was one of the three people in the world I was afraid of. Okay, that was a total lie. I was scared of a lot of people, but my grams, my mom, and my aunt Judith were the three witches on the planet that put the fear of the gods into me. And old Eloise was in this cabin, trying to seal up my death sentence all nice and tight, and I was in enough trouble as it was all on my lonesome.

"I'm not going anywhere with you."

Did that sentence actually squeak out of my mouth? Why, yes. Yes, it did. I even sounded confident and everything. But she'd waltzed in here without so much as a "how do you do" and demanded I leave with her, fully expecting me to peel my broken body off this damn couch and follow along like an obedient pup.

There were several reasons why I wouldn't be going anywhere with her, the chief ones being my ankle was probably broken, I had a *mother* of a concussion, and if I tried getting off this couch, Nico's head might actually explode. Plus, there was a good chance I would be getting kicked out of ABI selection school and then summarily executed in the next five minutes or so.

She might as well save herself the trouble.

Deputy Director Serreno eyed my grandmother like she was a troublesome stain or a petulant child she needed to quiet down. Her dark eyes surveyed the Bannister matriarch with a calculated glint. Without a doubt, she knew exactly who my grandmother was, and was trying to figure out just the best way to get her to shut all the way up and vacate the cabin as soon as humanly possible.

Nico, however, had a low growl building in his belly, and pretty soon, it wouldn't matter if my grams could blow him to kingdom come or if Serreno could arrest us all. The thought of anymore bloodshed was turning my stomach.

I mean I'd already been kidnapped and nearly launched off a mountain while trying not to get sold off to some dark Fae—named *Desmond*, for fuck's sake—and then watched a guy get his throat ripped out. I was topped up on drama for the rest of the day.

And by the way, what the fuck kind of name was Desmond, anyway?

"Excuse me?" I called, breaking the intense stare down between Nico and my grams as they both turned their gazes to me. "Oh, good, you've realized

I'm still in the room. I said I'm not going with you. I would like you to leave."

Look at me being all confident and shit.

I couldn't recall a single time in my life where I'd ever defied this woman, but today seemed to be the day for a lot of new shit.

Married? My gut churned. As far as I was concerned, marriage hadn't ever been on the table.

"And I would like to go a single week without one of your screw-ups, but here we are," she said, gesturing to the cabin itself. Eloise most likely found the place beneath her exacting standards. "Breaking into your instructor's home? Carrying on with this wolf? Sullying our name more than you already have? Really, Wren, are you trying to be this stupid or is it a honed skill?"

The sting of the insults sliced through my middle. She sure knew how to deliver a blow, my grandmother.

Nico's growl got louder, and he put himself further in between us, allowing me to school my features and wipe away the silent tear that tracked down my cheek. I could hug that man if I wasn't fighting off the urge to slap the shit out of him.

Married? Was he high?

"I wouldn't call it a screw-up," Serreno murmured, crossing her arms over her chest as she shifted her weight to her back foot. "Agent Bannister has displayed incredible fortitude and competency against a skilled and organized death mage, uncovered a black-market trafficking ring, and saved the life of one of her classmates in the process. I'm failing to see how you can find fault in any of those things."

Agent? For the second time in two minutes, I felt like bawling—only this time, it was happy tears.

Serreno tilted her head to the side. "I'm also failing to see how you were informed of any of your accusations at all. Especially without any of the actual facts. I'd love to know the name of your informant."

Oh, I had a guess, all right. Chet Ames was a bastard of the highest order. Since Girard was decomposing on top of this stupid mountain, there was only one instructor left that hated me. He'd been in my chili since day one, and if there was anyone who was going to tattle to Grams, it would be that asshole.

But... didn't he hate our family? Why would he willfully be in my grandmother's pocket?

Eloise adjusted the strap of her bag on her shoulder, the clinks of potion bottles and spell ingredients whispering like wind chimes.

"How I got my information is of no concern of

yours," she blustered, firming her jaw like she had a new adversary.

"Oh, I beg to differ," Serreno countered, a feral sort of smile widening her mouth. Nico had said she was a powerful elemental mage, but at that moment, she seemed like something else. "If information was leaked from this camp, not only is it my business, but I am also duty-bound to plug the leak."

Eloise sputtered, aghast that someone somewhere in this vast universe didn't give a flying fuck that her last name was Bannister. "You think you're going to throw your weight around with me?"

Serreno yanked a set of cuffs from her belt. "Not if you don't make me. But the way you're acting, I figure cuffing your ass will make my day."

Mashing my lips together, I did my best not to start cackling. Serreno was becoming one of my favorite people ever, and if she actually managed to cuff Grams? Well, it would make my whole year.

"Go ahead and try, mage. You have what? Maybe five years on me? That makes you practically a baby. You and your lapdog might as well be the ones cuffed."

Nico's growl rose on the air, and I figured we had about ten seconds before things got really dicey. Grams knew all about my predicament, but I couldn't remember if I'd explained to Serreno just how bad of an idea it was to use any sort of magic in my presence.

"You might as well give it up," I said, trying to defuse the situation. "I know who tattled, and you could get the phone records before she'd cough up a name. It was Ames. He's had it in for me since day one. It would have only taken a minor monetary contribution to make him rat me out."

I didn't bother looking at Serreno and I for damn sure wasn't going to look at Nico. Instead, I watched my grandmother's eyes narrow.

Yep, got it in one.

Granted, it wasn't much of a leap but still. It felt equally awesome to guess right and downright awful to know that my safety could be compromised so easily by a little money. Then again, I had almost been sold, so maybe that shouldn't have been such a shock.

"Do you care at all that I damn near died out there? That I ran for my life in the cold snow barefoot? That someone tried to sell me like I was property? Huh?" A flash of hurt and rage and... and I don't know what rippled through me so fast I thought I would explode.

Eloise's jaw hardened. *Yeah, I thought not.*

"So the only thing you care about is your silly

little name and your bullshit reputation. What else is new?"

"A reputation you tarnish by the second, carrying on with this wolf. This is by far the stupidest thing you've ever done. And darlin' girl, that's saying something."

I could have been a stain on the floor for as low as I felt. But what had Nico said in the shower what felt like years ago?

Fuck your family, Wren. Fuck every last one of them.

As much as I wanted to smack him upside the head for his "husband" talk, he sure as shit had been right on this front.

Fuck every last one of them.

"No, the stupid thing was ever believing I had a family. Why don't you do yourself a favor and forget I exist. And if you can't do that, well, then just fuck all the way off, Grandma."

With as much grace as I could muster—which wasn't much since I was a broken freaking mess—I climbed off the couch and stood tall, firming my jaw and my fist. And I couldn't believe the shit that was about to fall out of my mouth.

Gods, give me strength.

"I don't want to see you again. I don't want to see *any* of you *ever* again. I'm a drain on you and your name? Fine. You heard Nico. You can keep your fucking name. I have a new one."

Out of the corner of my eye, Nico's shoulders relaxed in what seemed like relief as a sigh gusted from his lips. Instantly, my hand was in his and he held it tight, and that made me feel like the biggest pile of shit in the universe.

Eloise staggered back a step like I'd slapped her, complete with a fluttering hand on her chest as if she was fighting off angina or something. "You wouldn't dare. If you're smart, you won't do this, Wren."

With my free hand, I pulled my collar to the side, displaying the crescent-shaped mark where my shoulder and neck met. Nico had bitten me over and over as we'd come together, the bites healing almost instantly, darkening with each new nip.

Tell me you want this. Tell me you're mine. Tell me you want me.

I hadn't known what he'd meant at the time, but now I sure as shit did. Those marks meant something big—something likely permanent—and I had been oblivious. And even if I didn't have all the details, pissing off my grandmother had become my sole priority.

"It's already done."

Her eyes zeroed in on the scar as her lip curled, her distaste clear. "You think you've got a target on your back already? It will be a thousand times worse once people get wise you've left the coven." Eloise huffed out a mirthless laugh. "But I guess that's your new family's problem now."

With that, she adjusted the strap of her bag and swept from the room, her nose in the air as she went. I couldn't help it, I flinched at the screen door slamming against the frame and yanked my hand out of Nico's hold.

Staggering backward, I plopped onto the couch, the rough motion jarring my head. Why had I said that to her? Just to stick it to my family? My gut churned with the ache in my head and the bitter lie in my mouth.

Because I wasn't Nico's wife—no matter what weird shifter claim he thought he had on me—and he wasn't my husband. I didn't have a new family or a new name.

Gentle hands cupped my jaw, tilting my head as Nico's soft lips brushed mine. Stupidly, I jerked my face out of his hold, the rough motion sending a sharp bolt of pain through my skull.

Understanding dawned in his eyes as a wince pulled at his lips.

"Married, Nico? *Married*? Have you lost your fool mind?"

Nervously, he rubbed at the back of his neck as he speared me with that hopeful look again.

"Don't you puppy-dog eye me," I scolded, holding up my left hand. "I don't see a ring on this finger or recall tiptoeing through the tulips wearing a white dress anytime in the last week. What. The. Fuck."

"Yeah..." Serreno broke in, "I'm going to step outside for a minute. Give you two some privacy."

Nico's boss hustled out of the room like her ass was on fire, that damn screen door making me jump once again as it slapped shut. If I had the power, I'd blow the stupid thing to smithereens.

But not once did my gaze leave Nico's nor did his leave me—a fact that was more and more uncomfortable now that his fists were stuffed into the very cushion under my ass, bracketing my hips, his eyes glowing with his animal.

Oh, but he wasn't going to Alpha his way out of this shit.

No way, no how.

"You have sixty seconds to explain," I threatened, holding up a hand with fingers ready to snap, "or we're going to see just how my magic reacts to null wards."

I was getting answers.

One way or another.

CHAPTER TWO

NICO

My mate was certifiable.

The glint of challenge in her gaze equally scared the shit out of me and turned me on all at the same time. It was tough not to drop my lips to hers, to not wrap her in my arms and bathe in her scent.

She was alive. Hurt, concussed, and probably emotionally scarred from the attack, but alive. At that moment, I didn't care that she was pissed at me, didn't give a single shit that she was threatening to blow us to kingdom come. All I cared about was the breath in her lungs and the steady beat of her heart.

"I'm waiting, Acosta," Wren growled, her jaw

practically granite. "And I've about had it with just about everything today, so cough it up."

It was a struggle to keep the grin off my lips. "Tell me what you know about wolf matings."

Her eyes narrowed. "Next to nothing, except that they mate for life." Her skin drained of color, bringing out the mottled bruises on her cheek and neck. "You're not telling me we're... that we're..."

Her breaths came in distressed pants, her eyes going so wide they showed white all around the irises.

With nothing for it, I dropped my lips to hers, gently brushing her mouth with mine before drawing back. "When a wolf is born, we're only given a fraction of our power. Some say it's so we don't mature too soon. Some say it's so we don't fuck around and kill ourselves before our frontal lobe develops. On a wolf's thirtieth birthday, we're gifted the remainder of our power, and with it, the call to our mate."

I kept my voice low, gentle. Wren needed gentleness right now.

"I got lucky," I murmured, cupping her face in my hands. "Most people search for their mate for years, decades, centuries. But I found mine before the turning, a freak chance that I happened to be at the right place at the right time."

Her gaze shifted from mine as chagrin twisted those beautiful lips. "The apothecary. Girard told me it was you who saved me."

Just his name had my blood boiling. Victor Girard was responsible for every mark on her beautiful skin, every cut, every drop of blood still crusted in her hair. His stink was on her even now, the cloying aroma of death magic and malice. And if I didn't have his blood under my nails, there would be no way I could stand it.

But he was dead, decomposing to ash somewhere up the mountain, and she was breathing.

And that's all that mattered.

Wren pitched her voice low as her gaze shifted to the window and then back to me. "He said yo-you killed two men—men he sent to kidnap me."

Oh, how my gut wrenched at the tremble in her voice. Wren had already witnessed just how brutal I could be. The absolute last thing I needed was her knowing everything.

Fucking Girard and his big, fucking mouth. It just figured he was the one to enlist those two fuckwads into snatching her.

"I did. Did he happen to mention that the men planned on raping you first before delivering you to him? You and your human friend."

Wren's face grayed out a little as she swayed in

her seat. Maybe I should have kept that bit under my hat, but I couldn't take it back now.

"Wyatt and I took care of it."

Her jaw firmed as she pulled from my grip. "And while I'm grateful, that doesn't excuse what you did —not the killing part," she amended almost under her breath. "The mating shit. Why didn't you tell me what it meant? It's my *life* you're playing with here."

And wasn't that just a punch to the gut? Standing, I put a decent amount of space between us. "I thought you knew. It wasn't until I was called away, did I realize that maybe you didn't. But you're from Savannah. You belong to one of the biggest witch families on the planet, for fuck's sake. I thought—"

Wren shoved to her feet. "You didn't *ask*. You *assumed*. You know damn well what assuming does."

"Yeah, yeah," I said on a sigh. "Makes an ass out of you and me." It was one of my father's favorite sayings, and I'd heard it far too many times for the damn thing to not stick. "I know I fucked up."

But somehow, I just couldn't bring myself to tell her I was sorry—because as much as I regretted taking her choice away—I wouldn't trade what I had with her for anything or anyone. Maybe it was the mating bond, maybe it was just Wren, but to me, it didn't matter.

"That's it?" she barked. "An 'I fucked up' is all you're going to say?" Wren tried to march around the couch, but she stumbled on her second step, hopping on one foot as she cradled her ankle, hissing in pain.

In all the commotion, I hadn't gotten a chance to leach Wren's injuries from her. Plus, I hadn't exactly done it while she was conscious before, so...

"How about," I muttered, scooping her up before my brain ever registered the movement, "you stay on the couch and just throw something at me instead?"

The connection that had led me to her while she was in danger sent a spike of pain through my skull and that ankle? Well, it was so close to broken it made me want to steal every ounce of agony from her so she never felt like this again.

"My skull's thick. It can take it."

"Damn right it is," she muttered, her voice like ice.

As soon as I got her settled on the couch, a pillow slapped me upside the head. I supposed I deserved that.

Sighing, I plucked the pillow from her fisted hands. "I want to tell you I'm sorry, but I can't," I admitted, meeting those green-gold eyes. In them was a fair amount of hurt—too much of it my doing. "That would imply that I am not fucking ecstatic at the hand I've been dealt. That would say that I'm mad at the universe for choosing you for me. And that would be the lie."

Wren squeezed her eyes shut, shaking her head. "You took my choice away, Nico."

"And for that, I am truly sorry. I didn't know I was stealing it, but I can't change it. And if it meant losing you, I can't say I would ever want to."

Instead of the hope or joy or anything positive I'd anticipated she'd feel, all I got was a wave of pain. Not physical—no, it felt like my heart was getting ripped from my chest. I pressed my hand against my sternum to stave off the ache.

"Jesus, what is it?" I asked, trying not to run to her. The last thing she'd want was me coddling her again. "Why do you feel like that? Why are you in so much pain?"

Wren's face practically turned purple as a wave of rage nearly knocked me over. "What? My emotions aren't even private anymore?"

A full mug of still-warm apple cider came sailing at my head, drenching me in the sticky-sweet liquid. Luckily, I managed to catch the cup before it made contact with my skull, but that seemed to piss Wren off more.

"Is anything just mine?" she shouted, launching another pillow at me.

This one I caught, too, but at the expense of the

mug. It fell to the floor, breaking into pieces, the sound making her jump. A fire burned in Wren's ribs —those fragile, bruised bones so close to broken it was a wonder she could breathe.

"Umm, guys?" Serreno called, poking her head in the door but smartly keeping her body on the other side of it. "I hate to interrupt this domestic you seem to be having here, but I'm going to need Wren."

"What now?" my mate growled under her breath, trying to school her features. Pasting a smile on her face, she turned to the door. "How can I help you, Director Serreno?"

Erica pressed her lips together in that way she did when she was about to ruin someone's day.

Ah, fuck. What now?

"Remember me calling you 'Agent' a few minutes ago? Well, I'm going to need to make that a reality. You're taking your ABI field exam. Today."

A wave of abject fear and a fair amount of nausea warred with acid churning in my gut. "How? She has four ribs bruised so bad they're damn near broken, a sprained ankle, a concussion, not to mention she nearly fell off a fucking mountain. You'd better have a good reason for this."

Another pillow bounced off my head, and I turned a glare at Wren.

"I can answer for myself, Agent Acosta," she

hissed before shifting to face Erica. "Is there a reason why this needs to get rushed? I'm not through with the course ye—"

Erica leveled us both with a half-irritated, half-sympathetic expression. "The Bannister matriarch has made a few phone calls in the wake of her departure. How she got service in the middle of this storm, I have no clue, but she has already contacted the council. If we're going to make sure she doesn't sink us all, I need you to be an agent as soon as possible."

Erica winced in a way that told me even this was going to be a stretch. "As in today," she continued. "With the way you just puked up ABI statutes, you'll be fine."

"But..." Wren's eyes widened as she felt for the necklace that was no longer around her neck. "I can't do the practical. I'll—"

"She'll do it," I said, cutting Wren off. "Give us a few more minutes, will you?"

Wren whipped her head in my direction, but I was already at her side, covering her mouth with my hand.

"Sure," Erica muttered, slipping back out the door before Wren bit the shit out of me.

"What the fuck, Nico?" she hissed under her breath. "First of all, don't you ever put your hand over my mouth again. Second, you know damn well I can't take that exam. I'll kill someone and probably myself trying to do those spells. What the fu—"

Rubbing at the crescent ring of teeth marks, I let a growl rumble from my chest. "You bit me."

"Pot," she hissed, pointing at her own crescent mark, "meet kettle. I can't take that test, Nico."

Kneeling, I got right in her space. "Oh, so I'm Nico again, huh? What happened to Agent Acosta?"

A fair bit of desire tempered the rage in her scent, but I couldn't do anything about that right now. "I wonder if I bend you over my knee and spank that ass of yours, you'll remember to call me Nico."

The jasmine and honey perfume of hers deepened, telling me she liked the words, even if she was pissed as hell at me. Fair.

"Don't get cute. I can't take that test no matter how good you are at distracting me. You swore you wouldn't let me hurt anyone. Please tell me I can at least trust that."

Even if I don't trust you.

She didn't say it, but she may as well have, and that sobered me far more than Serreno's interruption.

You should have asked her.

"I'll take care of it," I murmured, fitting my fingers under her chin and tilting it up. "I made you a promise—that you would make it out of here alive, that you wouldn't hurt anyone—and I don't ever intend on breaking it."

Without warning, I drew on my wolf—on the healing ability he so often lent to me—and pulled on the aches and pains littering my mate's body. The coppery tang of blood filled my mouth, but I kept on, allowing her to breathe easy for the first time since we'd made it off the mountain.

Wren's eyes went wide as the bruises faded from her skin. "I knew it," she breathed. "I knew it was you."

She was likely referring to the time I'd drawn her pain from her feet after Hell Night. Her poor skin had been hamburger by the time she was done marching all over this mountain, and I'd been so pissed she hadn't said anything. Now that I could feel her pain, I realized Hell Night had nothing on this.

Wren held down her agony so well, it made me wonder how many times she had told someone she was hurting, only to get brushed off, to get told to shut up. It made me want to rip her parents apart with my teeth.

"This ability that I have? It's a secret. There is only one other person in the world who knows about it other than you." Gritting my teeth, I swallowed down more and more of her pain. "I'm trusting you with the knowledge—knowledge that could get me killed if the wrong person found out—just like you trusted me."

"Nico," she whispered, but I shook my head.

"I don't have to be your mate or your husband. You're not a wolf, so you have the freedom to choose your partner and the life you want to live. I don't. The universe made the incredibly wise decision of picking you for me. But if this isn't what you want— if *I'm* not who you want—you can choose to not be my mate. But I am—irrevocably—yours."

Gently, I pulled my fingers from under her chin, brushing her lips with mine before I drew away.

"And if you're on the fence, just think of how good the angry sex will be."

CHAPTER THREE

WREN

Did that just happen?

Did Nico just turn me on, heal me up, and piss me off in one fell swoop?

Why, yes. Yes, he did.

Because instead of beaning him in the face with another pillow, I was imagining what angry sex would be like while also marveling at the fact that I could breathe easy for the first time in hours.

I'm trusting you...

I wanted to trust him—I did. I wanted to believe in kittens and rainbows and that today wouldn't take a solid turn into the shitter, but I'd already been kidnapped, beaten, and damn near fell off a mountain.

And it wasn't even dinnertime.

Now I needed to go take a test I was in no way prepared for, or else my grandmother was going to light the final match on my life.

But still, I was thinking about angry sex and Nico's growls in my ear and how good he could make me feel. Could anyone really blame me? Daydreaming about a hot shifter was far superior to impending doom.

"Thank you," I whispered, fighting off the urge to kiss him. He'd lied to me, he'd mated me or married me or whatever wolfy bullshit he'd done, and... Holding onto the rage was getting harder by the second—especially after he'd healed me.

"I'll get you a new null ward," he murmured, his eyes on my lips and his heat lowering my IQ points. "Keep my promise."

Shit. Had anyone ever kept their promises around me? Had anyone besides Ellie even made a promise at all? I was turning to goo again.

Get it together, girl.

But I flipped off my internal smart bitch and drifted closer to Nico, brushing his nose with mine. "I haven't forgiven you—not yet—but thank you. Again."

Then the day seemed to hit me all at once—being taken, running, falling, watching Girard get his throat ripped out—and shivers hit my whole body. I wanted to be strong—and I had been—but it was one thing too much. His kindness was too much. Even though he'd messed up, Nico still gave a shit. Warmth enveloped me as Nico wrapped me in his embrace, and with it, a level of safety I clung to like a drowning man.

"You've done so well, beautiful. You held yourself together so good," he murmured into my hair as he held me tight. "Most agents I know would have cracked by now. But I'm going to need you to be strong just a little while longer, okay? I'll even get you a new mug to throw at my head, yeah?"

Swallowing down the blind panic and fear at what my grandmother could be doing right now, I managed to chuckle wetly. "Good, but you should really shower. You're sticky and not in the good way."

Nico's irises flared gold with his wolf. "You're lucky I'm trying to be good right now." He leaned closer, his chest brushing mine as he whispered his threat. "Or else I'd turn you over my knee for teasing me. Play with your pretty pussy while I spank that ass of yours."

He drew back, and a rare smile pulled at the corners of his lips. "See? Told you angry sex would be fun. Just look at how flushed you are. Imagine how hot you'll be when I follow through?"

Jesus, Mary, and Joseph. Was it warm in here? And wasn't there something I was supposed to be doing? Staying mad at this man was going to be a challenge.

The man essentially married you under false pretenses, get your head on straight.

Oh, right. *Married.* That was the cold bucket of water I needed.

"How about you actually follow through with that null ward, and we'll just see who's getting spanked."

With that, I got up, steeling my spine as I marched past him. Nico wasn't the only one who needed a shower, and I would be damned if I was going to walk to the gallows with Girard's blood still on me.

"Where do you think you're going?"

Maybe it was the mild panic in his voice, but I stopped. "I'm getting Girard's stink off me and putting on clothes that haven't been tossed down a mountain. Is that all right with you?"

"But all your things are here. Dumond packed your things up after you were taken so Girard couldn't steal his scent off your stuff—not that he ever put his scent there, but..." Gently, he hooked his hand around my elbow, pulling me back toward the bathroom. "Take your shower. Be mad at me. Just... can you not leave, please?"

Swallowing hard, I managed to nod, and his gentle touch left me.

"I'll get your bag."

My bright-purple duffle made an appearance, stuffed full of uniforms and toiletries. I picked through it, nabbing what I needed before carrying the armload to Nico's bathroom. It was so high-handed and so freaking nice all at the same time that I wanted to throw my shampoo bottle at him.

I'd need to get that urge under control at some point.

Probably.

Without a word, I shut the door and turned on the tap, not bothering to look in the mirror. I didn't need to see the remnants of Girard's handiwork. Yes, Nico had healed me, but I knew the blood was still there, the dirt, the fear. When he had healed me before, I hadn't believed it. I'd figured I was dreaming, or it hadn't been that bad, or whatever nonsense I used to gaslight myself. But Nico *had* healed me, funneled my pain into himself as he leached it from me. Mended bones and scrapes, put my tattered skin back together.

And it hurt him to do it. It was like he felt my

pain as he took it from me, and that made my chest ache for some reason.

Hurriedly, I went through the motions of a shower without actually feeling any of it. Technically, I was clean, but that didn't take away everything that had happened or how sick I felt. As soon as Serreno could make it so, I'd be taking a final exam for a course I'd barely attended, all so my grandmother wouldn't have me locked up or executed or dragged back to Savannah by my damn hair.

Yippee.

A knock came at the bathroom door. "Wren, honey? You all right?"

I whipped that door open so fast an avalanche of steam billowed out of the bathroom to smack Fiona in the face. I hadn't seen her since Serreno hauled me to Nico's cabin for questioning. She appeared far better than the last time I'd seen her, all healed up by the med clinic and in fresh clothes.

Wrapping her in a hug, I was glad I'd managed to get dressed before her knock. "What are you doing here? Shouldn't you be resting?"

"And let you take that fool test by yourself? *Please.*"

Shoving her away, I gripped her shoulders with a

little too much gusto. "What? No. Please don't tell me Serreno is making you test out, too."

Fiona frowned before giving me a winning smile. "If I want the charges against Girard to stick and a real investigation to be had into this place, then the both of us need to be agents, Wren. It just makes sense for us to do it now. Plus, it'll be a snap." She waved a hand as if it was so simple as she plopped onto the edge of the couch. "Hannah told me you blew them out of the water during your practical."

But Fiona was forgetting a particularly important facet of that event—not that she was around for it, but whatever. Namely, the null ward I wore around my neck like my own personal good luck charm. It kept me from fucking up—kept everyone safe.

And to save us, I'd tossed it away. To save her.

How was Nico going to get me a new one? He didn't have time to trek down to Savannah and back. How was I going to pass this damn thing? Luck and blind optimism? I hadn't been lucky a day in my life.

"What about when Nico saved you?" Fiona replied to the thoughts I must have said aloud. "That seems pretty lucky to me. Of all the people to pull you from the burning wreckage of Azalea Apothecary, you got the super-hot shifter dreamboat with the giant dick and an unrelenting urge to keep you safe. If that ain't luck, I don't know what is."

"Whoa, who told you he had a giant dick?" Yes, that was what I latched onto, and yes, that sentence actually came out of my mouth.

Fi speared me with a sharp glare. "No one had to tell me that boy is packing a damn cannon in those pants. He just walks like he's got a monster in there. Like I told you before, I've got eyes, don't I?"

She wasn't wrong.

And now I was thinking of Nico's dick instead of how to escape this place before I blew it up. I really needed to sort out my priorities.

"Riddle me this, Obi Wan. How in the actual fuck am I supposed to do a practical exam without a null ward around my neck? You saw what happened on the range. That was unprotected. In case you missed it, I tossed the one I had so Girard didn't death magic you into oblivion."

Fiona winced. "Yes, that was unfortunate, but Instructor Smexy Pants is on the case. Though, you won't like who he had to bribe to get a new one."

Groaning, I skirted around her and plopped face-down onto the couch.

"It's that bastard, Ames, isn't it?" Yes, my voice was muffled in couch cushions, but Fiona heard me all the same.

"Got it in one," she said, smacking me hard on the ass. "Now get up, slap your hair in a bun, and let's get moving. Your grandmama is in a tizzy, stirring shit up so bad even my daddy has heard about it. The last thing I need is him moseying on over here before I have this shit handled."

That had me flying off the couch, wet hair smacking me in the face as I did so. "She told your dad?"

Josiah Jacobs was the Jacobs coven leader, and his method of rule was more like mob boss than President. If a Bannister had connections, he had *connections*, and all it would take is the right word, spell, or palm greased to get his nose all the way into our business. Though, considering a bunch of women were missing and there was a black-market ring selling them...

"Of course not." Fiona sighed, yanking me by the hand to the screen door. "Eloise Bannister giving my father a call? That would bruise her already-damaged ego. No, she got him word without *getting* him the word, if you know what I'm saying. He called a bit ago asking if I needed assistance."

Perfect. Just perfect.

Nico and his friend Wyatt sat in the two chairs on the cabin's front porch while a reluctant Ames stood several paces away. He held a golden necklace, brandishing it like it might ward off his impending doom.

Ames took a step forward but shuffled back three when Nico's snarl rumbled from his chest. "I told you to let her come to you. Don't think I've forgotten what you said to her, you fuck."

"And I told you that her grandmother filled my head with bullshit, man. How was I supposed to know she was lying through her teeth?" Ames flapped his hands, beaning himself in the head with the necklace as he went. "Everybody heard about her blowing up the apothecary. Shit, man, cut me some slack." He rubbed at the sore spot where the pendant smacked him, hissing in pain.

Ames had said some pretty shitty things to me in the week I'd been here—hounded me, humiliated me. And he wanted any of us to think it was just my grandmother's words that had done it.

Sure.

"What did she promise you?" I asked, pitying the poor bastard far more than I should. "I hope it was money and not respect. Eloise Bannister doesn't have respect for people she can manipulate, and you let her play your dumb ass like a fiddle. She doesn't give hand ups or handouts. She spins a web of words to make you do what she wants, and then hangs you out to dry." My laugh was mirthless. "Haven't you figured it out yet? The rumors are all true about her. *Duh.*"

If I'd been playing chess with the arcane world for two hundred and fifty years, a pissant warlock on the outs with his collective would be just the person I'd manipulate, too.

Grams was nothing if not consistent.

"But she said—"

"What? That I fucked around for grades? Or I was a menace to society and needed to be locked up? Or I was a vile little stain on the family name? I bet it wasn't that I got top marks in both high school and college. Or that I have a degree in chemistry and mathematics. Or that she hasn't been party to my life other than to tell me how big of a screw-up I am since I was a kid."

And all the while I was reading him the riot act, I was getting closer and closer. By the end, I'd snatched that damn amulet out of his hands, and had half a mind to beat him in the head with it.

Ames seemed both chastised and aghast. "Bu-but she promised she'd talk to my collective—get me reinstated. She said it would be a snap."

As if this joker needed to be near anyone with even a lick of power he could leach off of.

"She lied. It's what she's good at. If she does talk to them, it'll be to bury you. Loose ends and all that. Hopefully she's already forgotten you—that's the best-case scenario. Now, what does this thing do before I put it on? The last thing I need is another shitshow today."

The look on his face would have me pitying him if I didn't want to slap the shit out of him first. Ames shook himself. "It's a standard null. Nothing fancy. With the amplifying properties you have, you'll burn through it in a day. I'll make more. Send them with you."

"I'm sorry, what? Amplifying?"

"I mean, it makes sense why she'd want you back under her roof." Ames tapped his chin, a musing quality to his expression, which was a step up from the kicked puppy-dog one. "You probably fuel all their wards and spells. Who knows what'll happen if you leave for too long."

"What are you talking about? I'm not—" I shook my head, half-stumbling backward, the amulet swinging in my hand. "I'm not an amplifier. I'm a—" *Bane, albatross, perpetual fuck-up?* "—curse. Who told you that?"

"No one," Ames said, eyeing me like I was a special sort of stupid. "I saw the potion you made for Haynes. You cracked his seeing crystal even under two nulls. It's not rocket science. One plus one equals two. Totally makes sense why shit explodes around you. People are working with the wrong math, using the ambient magic like normal when you ramp it up to eleven."

He chuckled, shaking his head. "You're like a new moon, autumnal equinox, and a blood moon eclipse all wrapped into one. I'm amazed you've stayed under the radar as long as you have."

A pit of dread yawned wide in my belly. Hadn't that been what Eloise had said?

I had a target on my back.

Damn. I hated it when she was right.

CHAPTER FOUR

WREN

My breaths came in shuddering pants as I sprinted toward the berm that separated the testing area and the panel of judges that were grading my practical exam. Strapped to one thigh was a standard government-issue sidearm filled with sim rounds, and the other was a paintball gun filled with sleeping potion ampoules. Tied to my belt was a bag filled with witch tricks, potion bombs, smoke spells, and black salt—not that I'd be using any of that.

I was freezing, underdressed, and wildly unprepared for this shit.

My mission was to make it through a ramshackle

warehouse building, clearing it before apprehending the bad guy. And this was after my abominable showing at the written exam—complete with five essay questions.

Five.

With a minimum word count of three hundred words.

Each.

My brain was fried already, and I hadn't even done the hard part yet.

Truth be told, I was probably going to fail this shit. I had done exactly one day of weapons and tactics. One. And they wanted me to clear this building? By myself? Armed with a paintball gun, sim rounds, and a hope and a prayer.

I didn't care what Nico said, I was doomed.

Peeking over the snow-covered berm, I scouted the area. The coast was clear, but that didn't mean anything. There could be sigils under the slush, activating a circle that could blow me up. I didn't exactly trust the amulet around my neck. Ames' motives were questionable at best—though, if anything happened to me, I had a feeling Nico would rip him limb from limb in my honor.

Still, I liked my limbs right where they were, thank you very much.

It didn't matter how big of a pep talk Nico had

given me, I wasn't in the right frame of mind to be breaking into a building. But what were a few overused adrenal glands, right?

I supposed I could have stayed right there forever, commiserating my predicament, but a foghorn sounded, letting me know that the iteration had begun. I had to get through the warehouse, clear it, and apprehend the bad guy in under twenty minutes or I'd get dinged for each minute after the buzzer. With no time to waste, I crept over the berm, stalking toward the warehouse entrance like someone could come running out to kill me at any moment.

Which they totally could.

My mind raced with Ames' amplifier pronouncement. There was no way I was, right? No way I could be some kind of magical battery. He had to be yanking my chain because my grandmother screwed him over.

Though, his words made a sick sort of sense—especially since it meant that my whole family had been leeching off me my entire life. And wouldn't it make sense to keep me out of arcane spaces? Someone could find me out in a snap, right?

Shaking my head, I tried to focus on the problem at hand. Staying alive was the name of the game—not worrying about Ames' bullshit. Studying the entrance, I spied a sigil hidden in the graffiti plastered over the metal siding. It was a watching spell. Who needed digital cameras when all you needed was a spray paint can and enough power to fuel the mark?

Luckily, it appeared old, underpowered and fading—the first boon of the day. Still, I rummaged through the bag of witch tricks and yanked out the black salt. Salt was used for a lot of things, but black salt was for protection and breaking. I dumped a small pile of it in my hands and slapped it against the sigil, relishing the crackle as the marking faded into inert status.

One down, probably a million to go.

As an extra precaution, I dumped another little pile into my hands and blew it over the threshold before I breeched the building. Inside, it was a bevy of open space, rickety catwalks, and shoddy half-constructed rooms. And I'd have to clear them all. Aces.

After making sure the catwalks and obvious spaces were empty, I carefully opened the first room. Pitch black and full of debris, it took far too long to clear it. Maybe if they had put a flashlight in my pouch, it would have been different, but alas, I was stuck getting through the room by feel and the meager light from the open door. It took far too much of my allotted time, but I deemed the room clear and moved on.

The second room's entrance was around a rusty corner that had likely given someone tetanus at some point. A weathered nail protruded from the metal, covered in fresh blood.

Yep. Definitely tetanus.

As I skirted around the obstacle, a faint shuffling sound had me freezing to the spot, nearly snagging my shoulder on that damn nail. I drew my weapon, opting for the sleeping potion paintball gun rather than the Glock, and rounded the corner. I was met with a weapon of my own and a very familiar face behind it.

"What are you doing here?" I hissed at Malia, trying not to shout and give away our position.

She rolled her eyes at me, lowering her weapon. "Taking a test, silly, same as you."

"But—"

Malia shook her head. "We're running out of time. I'll fill you in later. Now, I've cleared those two rooms," she said, gesturing down the rusty, makeshift hall. "You?"

I pointed at the room behind me. "Just that one. Next hallway, you got my six?"

I'd always wanted to say that.

Malia's expression said she was having none of

this, but she'd humor me, anyway. Weapons drawn, we crept down the next hallway, keeping our eyes peeled for sigils and circles. Granted, that was hard to do given the debris and just filth all over everything.

Things were going well until a faint crackle sizzled through the air. A hand fisted in the back of my shirt, yanking me backward, right as a blade whizzed past where my face used to be. Wind swirled through the hallway, kicking up the trash and dirt, and revealing the sigil hidden under three pounds of grit.

Sand blasted our skin as arrows crisscrossed the corridor, embedding into the rust-covered walls. I looked back at Malia in thanks, but it wasn't just Malia standing there. No, next to her was a very crouched, yet not alarmed Hannah.

"You got anything in that bag that'll help?" the ghoul shouted, covering Malia as best as she could. If I had a guess, she'd been the one to yank me back, and I wasn't quite sure how to thank her.

I felt like an asshole for slipping out to Girard's cabin while she'd been indisposed, and even worse, getting nabbed on her watch. But that didn't matter right now. Passing this test did.

"Yeah, I got something."

Yanking out the black salt, I managed to keep a

small handful from blowing away in the maelstrom, but that wasn't the problem.

No, making it to the sigil without getting shot by an arrow with questionable origins was.

Just run, dive, and slap the salt on the sigil. Piece of cake.

Nodding, I'd managed to hype myself up enough to get moving when I was snatched back by Hannah again.

"What do you think you're doing?" she growled, her pale eyes glowing in the dim.

"I need to turn the spell off."

She let me go long enough to plant her hands on her hips and stare me down. "What's your plan on not getting shot?"

Other than running really fast, I didn't have one. But her hands were on her hips and not on my shirt, so I took that opportunity to haul ass. Three quick bounds and I dove, slapping the salt onto the very active sigil.

And hey, I'd only gotten one arrow graze for my trouble.

"Sweet mother of mercy, please tell me you did not just wade in here like a one-woman wrecking ball," a familiar voice hissed.

At this point, I wasn't even a little surprised to see Fiona emerge from one of the rooms, one hand holding her sidearm and the other gripping a potion bottle.

Considering she had approximately fifty arrows embedded in the door she'd just come out of, she should be thanking me, not griping, but whatever.

Getting up, I dusted myself off with a semi-bitter "You're welcome" and kept moving. I had no idea how much time this particular booby trap had wasted, but I didn't want to be on the other side of the timer—not if I could help it.

Between the four of us, we cleared the rest of the rooms in the hallway with little incident. Sure, the arm that had been grazed was hurting like a sonofabitch, but I'd power through. Personally, I'd have liked to rub black salt in the wound, but I didn't know if we needed to get through any more sigils.

Stop. You have a team now. You don't have to do shit by yourself.

"Hey, anyone have any black salt left?" I whispered, eyeing the next hallway from behind Hannah who had decided to take point.

I couldn't blame her. Out of all of us, she had the best hearing, sense of smell, and the most combat expertise. Fiona took the rear, watching out for any threats coming from behind.

Malia nudged the sore arm, and I fought off the urge to hiss. I took the still-full bottle from her and dumped a pile in one hand, slapping it against the open wound.

Yep, that stung like a motherfucker. Blistering-hot agony raced down my arm, and the oddest sensation of a spell breaking threaded through the limb. Oh, yeah, those arrows were tainted. I'd be willing to bet that rusty nail had been, too.

"Any of you cut?" I whispered through gritted teeth. *Shhhiiiitttt*, that salt burned.

I got negatives all around, so the fresh dripping blood on that rusty nail had to be from whoever we'd been sent in here to find. And they were already wounded.

With only one hallway left to search, we carefully went through it as a team. It wasn't until right before the last room did shit go utterly and completely sideways. At least this time, it wasn't my fault.

Oh, no. That honor was bestowed on Malia who crossed an active circle before either Fiona or I could stop her. The psychometry witch went flying, blown off her feet and into the closest wall by the force of it. In an instant, vines sprouted from the circle, latching onto Malia and drawing her in like she was a tasty snack to be gnawed upon.

Hannah and I dove for the small witch, keeping her from getting drawn in any further. Fiona kept her head, tossing a stunning potion bomb at the writhing vines. Unfortunately, all that did was make the spell defend itself.

Barbed spines shoved through the flesh of the vines, turning the hungry plant into a mace as it whipped this way and that.

"Use the salt," I yelled, fighting alongside Hannah to keep Malia outside the circle. I had no idea what would happen to her if she crossed it again, and I sure as shit didn't want to find out.

"Are they tryin' to kill us?" Fiona grumbled, tossing half the contents of the salt onto the circle.

Acid spewed from the thorns as the plant seemed to scream, the vicious liquid hissing as it landed on the dirty floor. A bit dropped onto my pant leg, eating through the fabric all the way to my skin.

And that would be the cherry on top of the shit sandwich of my day, but the fire of a handgun echoed through the rickety warehouse making the lot of us hit the deck.

Looks like we found our bad guy.

Sim rounds hit the metal wall with a not-so-comforting *plink, plink, plink*, the rounds ricocheting off the tin walls like ping-pong balls. That's when I caught a glimpse of blond hair.

Ames.

Gritting my teeth, I covered Malia and Hannah, who were returning fire with gusto, guiding them to cover before snatching the paintball gun from the holster at my thigh. Ames hadn't been hit yet, unfortunately, but I had a feeling his luck was about to change. Fiona abandoned her witchy trick bag in favor of a spell of her own, using the desiccating vines as a base.

A moment later, Ames was screeching like a harpy as the vines crawled up his legs. Gun and purpose forgotten, he batted at the slithering ropes like they were actual snakes. Then I gave into the urge I'd had since I stepped off the bus a week ago, firing round after round at the man until he fell.

I couldn't tell if the vines had tripped him or if the sleeping spell was taking effect, and really? I didn't give a shit. Every inch of exposed skin on the absolute worst instructor I'd ever met was doused in sleeping potion and the rest of him was trussed up like a Thanksgiving turkey.

"You know, I don't mind taking this test so much anymore," Malia said, her smile as vicious as her tone.

"Me either. Hannah, will you do the honors?" Fiona asked, staring at her watch. "We got two minutes before the buzzer sounds."

Hannah hoisted Ames up, tossing his vine-mummified body over her shoulder and hauling ass behind Fiona to the back entrance. The four of us piled out the building to the judges table, dropping the trussed-up instructor right at Serreno's feet.

A moment later the buzzer sounded, and the Deputy director's smile went wide.

Hope bloomed in my chest—well, that and Ames' amulet started burning my skin. Hissing, I pulled it from my chest without letting it go, praying no one noticed me as I moseyed on over to the null line and ripped the damn thing off before disarming myself.

Shit. Ames' amulet lasted less than an hour. There was no way I could rely on him to provide what I needed to stay safe.

"Congratulations, Agents. You have successfully completed the practical exam with flying colors. Each of you have passed the assessment and have been granted agent clearance. Because the four of you have worked so well together, I have decided to keep you all at the same duty location. I hope you like Savannah, ladies, it'll be your home for a while."

I passed.

I had half a mind to wilt to the ground and breathe the first sigh of relief I'd had since Nico had healed my ribs. Too bad the man in question had no intention of letting me wilt anywhere. A moment later I was swept up in warm arms, his shifter heat cutting through the chill of the night as he swung me around.

His lips found mine, his kiss warming me the rest of the way up.

"You did it, beautiful. You did so good," he said into my hair as he cupped the back of my neck.

Why was that a button for me? I swear he could get away with murder just kissing my hair and that little move.

"I watched you on the viewers. You took out the first one and we worried you'd take the rest out, too. You cleared every room, relied on your team. You got marks off for tripping the first trap, but you made up for it with the quick way you got out of it." Nico spun me in a circle. "Gods, babe, I'm so fucking proud of you."

Shit. Had anyone ever been proud of me like this? Ever? Maybe Alice. She'd been the only one to watch me graduate from college. She threw Ellie and I a joint party afterward. I wondered if she'd be proud of this, too.

"Thanks," I croaked, ducking my head to hide my face in Nico's shoulder, but his fingers found my chin, tilting it up to meet his gaze.

"Do you know how big of a badass you are? How well you did?" Gold shined bright in his eyes as he studied my face. "I know agents in the field right now who didn't come close to beating your score with years of tactical training."

I didn't know if I believed that. I'd messed up crossing a sigil and I should have seen the other watching spells. Plus, the null ward barely made it out of there. Twenty minutes of coverage? That wouldn't sustain me.

"I did okay. There are improvements I could make. Things to watch out for, bu—"

"Agent, you need to learn how to take a compliment," Serreno remarked, scaring the absolute shit out of me.

Smiling, I pushed out of Nico's arms. "Yes, ma'am."

I wouldn't say sorry because my mother and grams both hated it. *Don't say sorry, girl, get your head on straight.*

Yes, I was essentially three bags of trauma in a trench coat. So sue me.

She passed over a folded leather wallet with the ABI insignia embossed on the outside. I ran my fingers over the all-seeing eye bracketed by crescent moons. I'd thought this was impossible. Swallowing hard, I opened it, practically giddy at the gold shield and—

"What is this?" I whispered, staring at my college senior portrait over the name "Wren Acosta, Special Agent."

I didn't bother looking at Serreno. No, I stared at

the culprit, ready to throw this badge right at his head.

Nico's face paled a little, but he swallowed hard and soldiered on. "You said you had a new name, didn't you? Well, now it's official."

The only thing that was official was that I was going to fucking murder him.

CHAPTER FIVE

NICO

If I had a brain in my head, I would have told Serreno no when she said she was putting "Acosta" as Wren's last name in the system. At the time, I'd thought it was clever. No one knew who Wren Acosta was. No one was looking for her—especially not a dark Fae dealing in the black market. And with my name came all the protections of the Acosta pack—enough to deter just about anyone.

Even Desmond.

Plus, it would make her grandmother think twice about starting shit, along with anyone else who happened to have a grudge against the Bannisters or Wren herself. The apothecary debacle hadn't been the first time Wren had caused havoc, and most people didn't care that none of it was her fault.

Plus, all it would take was Ames opening his big fucking mouth, and the target on Wren's ass would double in size. Protection was a hot commodity right now.

But none of that seemed to make a difference as my gorgeous mate's eyes blazed with fury, her rage making it hard to swallow. It burned through my veins, a paltry echo of her own emotions.

"I said I had a new name—not that it was yours," Wren hissed, very aware of our boss standing two feet away, staring at us like we were adorable. "Of all the high-handed, patriarchal bullshit things for you to do right now."

Ouch.

Okay, she may have had a point on the patriarchal thing. Witches were inherently matriarchal. Male witches took the women's family name, foregoing their own, and gifts were usually passed through the mother's line. For Wren—or any witch—taking my name would be a legitimate sacrifice.

To throw my boss under the bus or to not throw my boss under the bus.

"It was my idea, actually," Erica announced, saving my ass. "The Acosta name offers certain protections within the Bureau that the Bannister name definitely does not. Your grandmother is doing her level best to start some shit, so the precaution is necessary. Plus, I can't station you two together if you're not registered as married in the system."

Aww, fuck. We were doing so well.

Wren pivoted on a heel to level me with the most scalding glare known to mankind before pasting a fake smile on her face and nodding, her voice the picture of a cultured Southern woman. "I appreciate your intervention then. If there's nothing else you need from me, I'll be heading to bed. Long day and all that."

Erica's smile was indulgent at best. "Of course. Congratulations, Wren. You really have done a phenomenal job. The ABI is lucky to have you."

Erica didn't hand out compliments—no matter if they were kind or not—so the praise was indeed genuine. Wren's head dipped in thanks before she spun, marching toward the cabins without a word. Yep, I was fucked and not in the good way— especially since she started heading for her old cabin instead of mine.

My fingers found themselves at her elbow before I could blink. "Where you going, Wren?"

The absolute last thing I could take was her not being safe. I needed that more than I needed air.

"Away," she growled, yanking her arm out of my grip.

I didn't touch her again, but I did step in front of her before she could take another step. "Please," I murmured, holding up my hands for her to stop, "don't take Erica's caution as another strike against your freedom. I know it stings, but I want you to see—"

Wren's badge smacked me in the face, the hard metal shield catching me in the forehead. "A strike against my freedom? A *strike* against my *freedom*? You don't know the first damn thing about me if you think I'm just going to let you railroad me into anything, Nico Acosta. I'm going to my cabin by myself, and I'm going to bed by myself, and I'm going to Savannah. By. My. Self."

There was a problem with all three statements, namely that none of those things were true.

I bent, snatching her badge from the ground, and in my distraction, Wren skirted around me, marching double-time to her cabin.

Welp, in for a penny, in for a pound.

Catching up to her in no time, I put a shoulder into her belly and lifted her over my back. Wren screeched as I adjusted course, heading for my—or rather, Wyatt's—cabin.

"You put me down right now," she ordered, but I was doing no such thing.

I'd tried sleeping without her last night, and that didn't work, and after the events of the previous twenty-four hours, there was no chance in hell I'd be trying it again tonight. Plus, the woman needed healing. Again. Already. The remnants of an acid burn and poison from a dart still coursed through her tired body.

We passed Wyatt on the trek to his cabin, the big man trying not to laugh at our antics as he polished a bright-green apple on his plaid jacket. "You're sleeping somewhere else tonight."

What had Wren called me? High-handed? Well, I was an Alpha, and I needed that cabin more than he did right now.

"I figured," Wyatt said before biting into the apple. "Good luck, buddy."

I'd fucking need it. Wren kneed me in the chest and elbowed me in the back. I'd need to teach her how to get out of this hold later, but for now, I needed her in a space—any space—with me. Preferably sans clothes, but I'd take what I could get.

In no time, I was back at the cabin and had Wren inside and out of the cold. She'd gone into that broken-down building without a coat, minimal weapons, and thin body armor. Hell, if she weren't so mad, she'd actually feel it, too.

Reluctantly, I readied myself to set her down, knowing full well I might not get to touch her again for some time. Sliding her body against mine as I soaked in the last bit of her, Wren found her footing. My feet unwilling to move, only let me take one slight shuffle-step backward, her scent, her heat, her fire the only thing keeping me sane.

I held out her badge. "You worked hard for this. You earned it. I know you didn't want my name, but you have it and all the protection it provides. You have an entire pack at your back, Wren. Please understand what that means."

Her lip curled as she snatched it from me. "It's another bullshit yoke, is what it is. *Don't be stupid, Wren. Don't talk so much, Wren. Go somewhere else while the adults in the room talk, Wren. Mind your manners, Wren.* It's another family being disappointed in me and me failing to measure up. It's another leash. And I get it. I screw up all the time with this wonky shit in my veins. Get wild hairs up my ass about whatever, but this was something I could do that was just mine." She swallowed hard, the wounded child peeking out from behind the rage in her eyes. "Nothing is mine anymore."

Her words had me taking a step back.

"Everything is yours. Everything. My pack is yours, my family is yours, my heart is yours. You earned that badge—not because of me, but in spite of me. Serreno doesn't give compliments. She sure as shit doesn't care if you've had a bad day. You impressed her and those judges. That badge is an honor, and you earned it all on your own with only a week of training. Don't you understand just how fucking rare that is?"

Unable to stay back another second, I crowded her, herding her to the closest wall so I could pin her in. "And my family is nothing like yours. We love each other. We care about each other. Just like every family, we have our problems, but not a single member would disrespect you the way your family has. Not one."

Wren's eyes blazed as she stared at my mouth.

"And my heart, my life, my soul, my happiness, my cock, my pleasure. All yours. You own it all, my beautiful bird. Don't you know that?"

Her head tilted as her gaze went heavy-lidded. "Prove it."

Her scent rose on the air, that honey and jasmine perfume of her desire. *Gods, I was doomed.*

"How would you like me to prove it? You want to tie me up while you make yourself come on my cock? You want me on my knees? Tell me, beautiful. How do you want me?"

A devious smile pulled at her lips as her heart picked up speed. Want flooded our connection, ramping up my own. I'd said something she liked, I knew that much, and I couldn't wait to sink into her now that there wasn't a null ward between us.

"Strip," she ordered, a lovely thread of power in her words. Wren didn't know it, but she was tapping into me just as much as I was her. "I want you naked."

At the command, I did exactly what she wanted, toeing out of my shoes as I peeled off my jacket and shirt, unbuckled my belt, and slid my pants off. Now only in boxer briefs, I stood before her, arms wide, loving the caress of her gaze skating over my flesh.

"Underwear, too. I want to see that beautiful cock of yours."

"Far be it for me to deny a lady," I replied, hooking my thumbs into the waistband and slipping out of them."

Her breaths quickened as she licked her lips. What I wouldn't give to have those lips on my cock right now.

"Tell me you have some rope in this place." A fire burned in her belly, blotting out reason and doubt, singing through the link we shared.

"Sorry, beautiful, I don't. I do have a few pairs of handcuffs, though."

Her eyes lit with joy as her smile turned sultry. "Perfect. Bring them to me."

Gods, Wren in charge was going to do me in, and we hadn't even gotten started yet. Like the obedient mate I was, I retrieved the cuffs and handed them over.

"You're doing so good, baby," she cooed. "Now lay down on the bed, arms wide."

So, tying me up, then. As long as I got her, I didn't give a shit what I had to do. Plus, Wren in charge was fucking phenomenal. Following her lead, I laid down, spread eagle, waiting for her to slap those cuffs on my wrists.

In a few twists of her wrist, I was secured to the headboard, the cuffs tight but not uncomfortable.

"You going to give me a show, beautiful?" I asked, watching as Wren peeled off her body armor and top.

"That depends," she replied, shimmying out of her jeans and boots, "on if you can be patient. I need a shower, and you're going to stay right there and think about what you've done."

"Wren," I warned, pulling at the bonds.

"*Nico,*" she responded, her words teasing. "I'll just be a minute."

Then she walked her sexy ass past me to the

bathroom and shut. The. Door. Oh, I was spanking that perfectly plump ass just as soon as I got free.

Thirty minutes later—and yes, it was thirty because I watched every second of that clock—Wren emerged from the bathroom, her hair wet and piled on her head, her skin flushed with the heat. Her scent flowed through the cabin, greeting me before she did. Her sexy curves hidden by a towel, she stood next to me, a single eyebrow raised.

"You still want me?" she murmured, a seductive husk to her voice. Gods, this woman could do me in with a single question.

My gaze drifted down to my very proud, very erect cock and back to her face. "I think you know I'll always want you. But right now? I want you more than I want air."

Lust bloomed through our connection, nearly knocking me for a loop.

"That's good. You know, I almost touched myself in the shower without you," she admitted, opening her towel and showing me her perfect skin. "Almost made myself come all over my fingers just thinking about you tied up out here."

She threw a leg over mine, straddling me, my cock mere inches from Heaven. But did Wren even graze my aching, leaking head?

No. No, she did not.

Instead, she held herself from me as she grazed her own skin, palming her breasts, plucking her already-tight nipples.

"Fuuuucccccckkkkk," I groaned, shifting restlessly on the sheets, trying for just a brush of her sex against mine. The pleasure she was giving herself threaded through me—enough that I was ready to rip out of these cuffs and take her over my knee.

Her hands traveled down her stomach, her fingers threading through her auburn curls. "Just like this," she said. "But I thought you'd want to see me. And you want to, don't you? Watch me fuck myself?"

My mouth was as dry as the Sahara. "Yes," I croaked. "I want to see everything."

She whimpered as she grazed her clit with her thumb, fucking that sweet pussy with her fingers, her delicious heat so far out of reach.

"Let me taste you," I ordered, the thread of command thick in my voice.

Wren raised an eyebrow, not giving an inch. "Good boys say please, Nico. Everyone knows that."

"Please," I whispered, needing her taste on my tongue. Needing it, craving it. If she was going to torture me this way, I wanted something, anything of hers.

Wren's smile widened as she crawled up my body,

grazing her luscious tits up my belly and chest. I tried capturing a nipple in my mouth, but she kept it just out of reach. She straddled my chest, her wet, slick heat so close and so far—all at the same time. I wanted her to sit on my face, wanted to lap her up, and drink her down.

Wanted her pleasure for my own.

But instead of letting me taste her, she went back to work, milking herself of pleasure just out of reach. Her scent filled my nose so much I could almost savor her sweetness, and as her pleasure ramped up, it got thicker in the air. She let her hair down, the wet strands curling over her gorgeous tits as she writhed. She plucked at her nipples, making herself hiss in desire.

"That's it, beautiful," I growled. "Make yourself come all over my chest. Fuck that gorgeous pussy."

My words must have done the trick because Wren went off like a bomb, her orgasm slamming into both of us, nearly taking me over with it.

But she didn't come to me, didn't press her body against mine, and that's when I decided I'd had about enough of this shit.

A flick of my wrists later, and Wren was on her back in my bed, her eyes wide. I nearly hissed at her warm skin against mine, but I was too preoccupied with her surprise. It was fucking adorable.

"Yo-you just broke out of... How did you... How strong are you?"

Like a pair of steel cuffs were a match for any shifter, let alone an Alpha. "Sweetheart, I'm an Acosta Alpha, next in line to take my father's place if he ever decides to step down. A shifter is strong. *I* am stronger. Now, you've had your fun. It's my turn."

Her wide green-gold eyes flared as her mouth parted, and even though she'd just had an orgasm, Wren's desire blazed through us. As reluctant as I was to move, I shifted the both of us, hauling her over my lap with her perfect, luscious ass presented to me like a present. As I ran my palms over her skin, she shivered—our connection, her recent orgasm, and her need making every inch of her skin something for me to play with.

And I was going to play.

Like a whip, my hand struck, spanking her perfect peach of an ass. Wren moaned as a bright-red palm print bloomed across her pale flesh.

"So fucking pretty," I growled, rubbing over the mark before striking again in a new spot. Her new moan was music to my ears. "I bet you're dripping now, aren't you, beautiful?

"Answer me." I struck again right where her ass and thigh met, so close to her exposed pussy I bet she could feel the displaced air before the hit. This time her moan was louder, needier. The orgasm she'd had was barely a memory now.

"Yes," she whispered. "I'm so wet. I need you."

Slipping my fingers through her folds, I pushed two inside her slick heat, relishing how she soaked my fingers.

"Tell me who I belong to, Wren," I ordered, grazing my thumb over her clit. "Who owns me?"

"I... I do," she moaned, shifting her weight to her knees.

With my other hand, I fisted it in her hair, arching her back as I fucked her with my fingers—or rather as Wren fucked herself on my fingers. Swiveling her hips, she stole her pleasure, rubbing her clit against my thigh for added stimulation.

"Who owns this cock?"

Oh, but my sweet mate wasn't going to steal another drop. Pulling my fingers from her, I spanked the other thigh, her moan louder, longer, more desperate.

"Answer me," I growled, spanking her again.

She fisted her hands in the comforter, whimpering at the loss. "I-I do."

"Damn right you do." I sat back on my knees in the bed, moving her so she straddled my thighs again, her back to my front. Her warm skin kissed my chest, her trembling, needy breaths threading through me.

"You want my cock, beautiful?" I murmured, one hand plucking at her already-tight nipple and the other sliding through her slick folds.

"Yessss," she hissed, her hips bucking with need. "I want it."

Collaring her throat, I steered her face to mine, taking those lips for my own. Our tongues met, her desire ramping up with each second I denied her. But I couldn't hold back anymore. Abandoning her clit, I guided my cock to her opening, sliding into her with one slow stroke.

Wren moaned in my mouth, her hips bucking so hard, I had to hold her across her belly just not to lose her. She slammed herself back down onto my cock, finally taking her pleasure from me.

"That's it," I whispered against her lips. "Be a good girl and fuck me like you own me."

And she did, she slammed down on me, like any second now I'd take my cock away from her, and all the while, I took that sweet mouth, played with her clit, and relished the moans that vibrated from her throat.

"More," Wren whimpered. "I need more." Meaning, she needed me to take over.

"Good girls say please, Wren," I chided, parroting

her earlier words as I pulled her off me, flipping her to her back. "Everyone knows that."

Her hips bucked in impatience, but I still got my "please."

Then I was inside her again, thrusting hard enough to make her whimper.

"Who do I belong to, Wren?" I asked once I felt her tighten around me, her orgasm so close it was like my dick was in a vise.

Her chest flushed, her eyes glowing with her pleasure—and a fair bit of magic—her lips wet with my kisses, she never looked so beautiful.

"Me," she whispered on a moan, her legs banding around my back so tight I could barely breathe.

"Who do you belong to?" I asked, slowing my rhythm, circling my hips to put pressure on her clit. "Tell me."

She bit down, those perfect white teeth indenting her plump bottom lip. "You."

I needed that whispered word more than anything. It was forgiveness and permission all at the same time. My fangs lengthened, the wolf under my flesh barely leashed, and I struck, burying them into her neck as my thrusts picked up speed. Wren's orgasm hit almost immediately, taking me down with her.

Heat raced up my spine, tying us together tighter

than we had been before. Her emotions came through more, her heartbeat in my chest, her breaths in my lungs. I kissed her then, her blood still in my mouth, sharing the coppery nectar like it was ambrosia.

"There's no getting rid of you now, is there?" she teased, nipping at my bottom lip.

"Nope. You're stuck with me."

I had a feeling she didn't mind.

Not one bit.

CHAPTER SIX

WREN

Waking up before the sun wouldn't be such a bummer if I always did it in Nico's arms. Warm and safe and delicious, we smelled of passion, a fair bit of sex, and blood. The coppery tang had never been so strong before, and I found it strange that with just a little bit spilt the night prior, I could still smell it now.

And if the shifters or ghouls got a whiff of me, they'd know exactly what we'd been doing all night—not that it mattered much anymore. I had a feeling word had gotten around about my and Nico's relationship, and if that didn't do it, the giant crescent bitemark on my shoulder would be a dead giveaway.

It had changed sometime in the night, too. Instead of the faint line it had been, the scar was thick, silvery, and nearly glowed in the dim light of the bathroom. I'd gotten out of bed to use the facilities and scrounge some breakfast, but stopped in my tracks at the reflection of the bite in the mirror. I'd remembered him sinking his fangs into my neck, sure, but it hadn't hurt enough to make this scar.

Had it?

The faint aftershock of the orgasm had my sex clenching. No, that bite hadn't hurt one bit. Smiling, I took a quick shower, and hopped out. I was under the impression we were leaving today to report to the Bureau, and we'd need to get a move on. I tossed on a pair of leggings and a tank, stealing a flannel from Nico's bag. Sure, I could wear something of mine, but I wanted something of his on me now that I'd washed off his scent.

Weird wolfy mating bullshit.

After tying my shoes and slapping a beanie on my sex-mussed hair, I was super bummed to find only beer, lunchmeat, bottled water, and—of all things holy—*pickled beets* in the fridge.

Coffee was required for a morning such as this.

And *food.* I was hungry enough to eat my weight in bacon, but I'd settle for whatever was available. Quietly, I slipped out of the cabin, making sure the screen door didn't slam against the frame and cut through camp to the dining hall.

The place was mostly empty, only a few line cooks still behind the salad bar-style stations. I had no idea what time it was, but the containers were full of all the good stuff, so I snagged a tray and a couple of to-go boxes and started filling. By the time I was done, I had double the food I could usually eat, plus some. It might not be enough for a shifter, but it was the thought that counted, right?

I was in the middle of getting the coffee when the faint trace of Fiona's perfume hit my nose and a hip bumped mine, making me bobble the empty coffee cup in my hand. Miraculously, I didn't drop it, snatching it out of the air before it hit the now-dirty floor. I'd cleaned this place good enough to eat off that floor not two days ago, and it was already trashed.

Ick.

"Oh, girly. You look positively rumpled," Fiona said, not scandalized in the slightest. "Nico's buddy Wyatt said he saw Instructor Smexy Pants toss you over his shoulder after the test. It looks like you got the *good* business last night."

It would be tougher to deny everything she just said if every bit of it weren't one hundred percent true. I shot her a conspiratorial smile and poured myself some coffee. I did get the good business and then some. The way Nico gave himself over to me, letting me know he was mine... I got the shivers just thinking about it.

"Good morning, Fi. How did you sleep last night?"

By the looks of her, Fiona hadn't slept a wink, though I couldn't say I blamed her. She didn't have her own personal wolf to keep the bad dreams and boogeyman away.

"I'll sleep better once we're out of here. You didn't stay for the briefing, but we're headed back to Savannah today. We have the rest of the week off, though, and report back next Thursday. Serreno gave us time to find a place, get settled."

That sure was nice of her. Though, I didn't know how settled I'd be with no money and no place to live. Carmichael Jones had taken every red cent I'd ever earned, and now I was on the outs with my family. I supposed I could stay with Ellie, but her house was so small, it really would be an imposition.

"Luckily, Dad already snagged me a place. When he heard that all four of us passed and got stationed together, he snatched up a four-tier row house. Each of us get our own floor—that is, if you want to stay with us. I know you got a hot man who probably has a pack house on standby, but..."

Pack house? Hell, no. I couldn't imagine living in a house full of strangers, let alone meeting Nico's family. I knew it was coming with all the marriage and mate talk, but... The only mom who'd ever liked me was Ellie's and that was because Alice loved everyone. Any boyfriend I'd ever had in the arcane community—and the term "boyfriend" was a stretch —never wanted me to meet their parents. Never even wanted to be seen in public with me, and the human ones?

Ugh. I didn't even want to think about it.

There was no way I'd be walking into the Acosta pack house for Nico to tell his parents he got stuck with the Bannister albatross. *No, thank you.*

"I want the place," I answered, excited for the first time since forever. A place to live that wasn't anywhere near my parents. *Sign me up.* I wasn't sure how I'd pay for it yet, but I'd figure that out soon enough. "Where is it?"

I didn't have a car, so I hoped it was within walking distance of the ABI building.

"I think it's near something called Chatham Square? Here, I've got pictures," Fi said, handing over her phone. She must have gotten it back upon graduation.

Chatham Square was a block-sized greenspace, chock-full of Fae portals in the middle of wolf central and the witch territory. Granted, it wasn't far enough from my parents' house for my liking, but it was close to the ABI building. Scrolling through the pictures, though, I fell in love—especially with the ground-level apartment.

"Hannah and Malia picked their apartments, but I wanted to let you choose yours."

Blinking, I handed her phone back. "I couldn't. You pick, and I'll take what's left. And how much do you want for rent? Utilities? I don't have much right now, but I can get you money just as soon as we get paid."

That was a total lie. I didn't have two pennies to rub together, and I had no idea when we would be getting paid by the ABI. And just by the pictures alone, the place looked like it would cost in the millions. Even if I *could* pay rent, I might not be able to afford what she'd charge. Hell, knowing that, Fi might not want me as a roommate at all.

Fiona stared at me like I was two pickles shy of a full jar and snatched the cup from my loose fingers. "Girl, you put your ass on the line to save me.

Hannah and Malia told me you were the one pushing to know more, to get Nico involved, to..."

She shook her head, her eyes welling up as she filled the cup with hot coffee, shifting her body so I couldn't see her face anymore. "I wouldn't be alive if it weren't for you." By the time she turned around again, her face was a calm mask. "Plus, I own the building," she said, offering a little shrug and handing over the full cup. "You don't pay rent. *Ever.*"

Blinking, I half-stumbled away from her in shock, nearly sloshing hot coffee over the rim. "But... I didn't... you shouldn't..."

Fiona rolled her eyes and waved her hand in mock defeat. "If you need to feel like you're contributing, you can chip in on utilities, but honey," she said, her eyes shifting around to make sure no one was in earshot, "I don't need the money. We'll get your apartment all warded up nice and tight, I just need to know which one. Hannah picked the street level, Malia the one above it. I was thinking of taking the top one because of the clawfoot tub, but I—"

"I'll take the ground," I said in a rush.

I absolutely adored the ground floor apartment. Sure, it had the most risk of flooding, and it was essentially a studio, but the walls were thick stacked stone, and it had the walkout to the courtyard. Plus, it had the best kitchen.

I'd always wanted a kitchen to myself where I could cook meals I wanted, without my mother's disapproval. Margot Bannister was rail thin and hadn't ever met a calorie she didn't despise—or chastise anyone else for enjoying. Hell, she didn't even season her food. All the flavor in Savannah, all the culture, and my mother couldn't be bothered to put anything spicier than pepper on her plate. Alice Whitlock, however, had taught me how to cook when I was eleven, and I'd always had a passion for it.

"Well, then that's settled. Oh, and you should check your bank. I've already gotten my signing bonus and my first check from the ABI and then some. Probably a bit of hush money for getting kidnapped by an instructor and everything, but I'll take it."

I shrugged. "I don't have my phone yet." I knew for a fact I didn't have a signing bonus and I was just lucky to get out of here without dying. "I'll check later. When are we leaving?"

Fiona checked her watch. "About an hour. Dad sent a car for us, so we don't have to ride that damn bus down the mountain. I don't know about you, but that was the worst ride of my life, and I don't intend on a repeat. Want to come with us, or is Instructor Smexy Pants going to toss you over his shoulder again?"

That brought me back to reality. I hadn't intended on being gone so long. "No idea. I'll come find you in a bit. And..." I enveloped her in a hug. "Thank you for everything."

After bidding our goodbyes, I finished pouring the coffees and headed back to the cabin. I'd need my phone at some point and to check my bank account. The apartments seemed to be furnished, but that could just be staging. I'd need to see how much I had in case I needed furniture.

Plus, all I had to my name was in my purple duffle. Just the thought of going back to the Bannister Manor and snatching my things sounded like a great way to get myself cursed or locked up or worse. If what Ames had said—and I still didn't know if I believed him—was true, then getting out would likely cause a shitstorm I didn't want to deal with.

I'd stacked the coffees one on top of the other, slightly bumbling the to-go boxes as I tried to open the screen door, when the damn thing popped wide, nearly knocking me on my ass. Somehow, I didn't drop anything but the top coffee—that was mostly empty—the remnants splattering across the porch planks.

I was met with a shirtless Nico, his jeans half-buttoned and slung low on his hips. His eyes glowed with his wolf, his breaths coming in distressed pants.

"Where have you been? I woke up and you were just gone."

My eyes narrowed. *Oh, no.* No, he did not just walk out of that cabin half-dressed and have the audacity to ask where I've been. I was not a five-year-old who needed adult supervision. Gritting my teeth, I passed over his coffee and breakfast, which was all the answer he was going to get.

"We're leaving in an hour," I said, skirting around him with my own breakfast. "Do you think I could get my phone back from the amnesty box? I'd like to call Ellie and check my bank account."

"Wren," he called to my back as I rummaged through the drawers for a fork. "Answer me."

He even used that Alpha tone that made everyone within a mile radius want to fall to their knees. Funnily enough, it didn't work on me right then.

"I don't have to *answer you*, Nico." Rolling my eyes, I stuffed a pancake in my mouth, still irritated I was missing out on the rest of my coffee.

"The fuck you don't," he insisted, moving closer,

his shoulders seeming to get wider, his body bigger. "You can't just—"

Swallowing, I cut him off. "You're holding hot coffee and breakfast. Where the fuck do you think I've been?"

This was not the start of the morning I wanted. I'd wanted to get us breakfast and continue the smoochy, lovey-dovey post-sex bliss we'd had all night. But *noooooooooo*. I got grumpy Nico who most definitely should not look that hot when being that big of a dumbass.

Nico blinked, finally staring down at the food in his hands. "Oh."

I swallowed another bite, this time bacon. "Yeah. *Oh*. I don't know who you think you are, but my daddy ain't it. I get it—with everything that happened—I'm a little on edge, too. But damn, man. You made me spill my coffee. That's just straight blasphemy."

He finally had the good sense to appear ashamed of himself. "Yo... you left the cabin without my wolf alerting me. You took a shower, and I had no idea. The only reason I woke up at all was because the bed was cold with you gone. I thought—"

But he didn't finish his sentence. Instead, he passed over his cup and kissed me on the forehead. "Thank you for breakfast."

His fingers drifted down to the neck of my—or rather, *his*—shirt. "I like this. A lot."

I just bet he did. "That I'm wearing your shirt or the giant glowing bitemark on my neck?"

"What?"

Nico hooked a finger in the collar to inspect the marking. Honestly, I was surprised Fiona hadn't said anything about it.

"It took," he breathed, marveling at what I'd already studied in the mirror. "I can't believe it. You really have an Acosta mark even though you aren't a wolf." Nico pressed a feverish kiss to my lips. "Do you know how fucking special this is? I'm the first wolf in four centuries to mate outside our class, and you took the mark beautifully."

I coughed, choking on my pancake. "What?"

Instead of answering, Nico kissed me again, but I pulled away, scrabbling to standing before either of us could blink. "So, you're telling me that not only am I a witch freak, but I brought your ass down with me?"

"No—"

Sure, I was still mad about the marriage bullshit but... "And you didn't think to mention that shit yesterday?"

Nico lifted his hands in surrender. "It's not a big

deal. We'll go to the pack house. You'll meet my family. It'll be fine. They'll love you."

The laugh that came out of my mouth was pure hysteria. No family—save for Ellie's—had ever loved me, and there was no way a pack as big as the Acostas—with their proud lineage—wouldn't hate an Alpha mated to a witch. Especially this witch.

Not just hate it.

Despise it.

"The fuck we will. No. No way. Nuh-uh. Never. Not in a million years. Absolutely not."

I abandoned my breakfast and practically dove for my duffle. At this point, I figured fuck the phone, but a flash of light blue plastic caught my eye. Breathing a sigh of relief, I held onto the thing like my life depended on it.

"There is no way on this earth I'm meeting your parents, Nico. I have known you for a week. A week. And now you drop this bomb?" Shaking my head, I yanked the bag onto my shoulder and started heading for the door. "*It's not a big deal. It'll be fine,*" I mimicked, snatching up my badge from the counter.

"I'm going with Fiona, Malia, and Hannah. Fi has room for me."

"Wre—"

"No, sir. No. You had all the time in the world to drop that bomb and you chose to keep it under your hat. You can go to the pack house and tell them whatever the fuck you need to tell them, but your ass is going by yourself."

Nico latched onto my elbow, but a snarl ripped up my throat so fast it scared the both of us. I didn't snarl or growl or whatever noise wolves used. But I'd used it then.

Nope. No. I am putting that shit on the back burner, and we are thinking about that round about never.

By the time I made it to the cabin, I'd managed to paste a smile on my face. Twenty minutes later, I was in a luxury SUV tooling down the mountain. Six hours after that, I was stepping foot in the first home that hadn't been Ellie's or my family's in my life.

Ten minutes after that, I was staring at a very shirtless Nico who was sitting propped up against the pillows in my new bed.

Of course he was.

So much for getting the last word.

CHAPTER SEVEN

NICO

My mate was doing my head in.

First, it was the perpetual clumsiness—which I found adorable, if not a little frightening. Then, it was the death sentence hanging over her head. We seemed to be on the other side of that at the moment, but the threats just kept on coming. There was something lurking in the shadows, just waiting to pounce, and I couldn't figure out how to let her know that we weren't out of the woods yet.

Plus, there was another problem—one I hadn't expected.

Namely, that she was exhibiting some brand-new

wolf characteristics that I wasn't all too comfortable with.

My bite's effect on her had been unexpected. But the glowing eyes, the snarling, the aggression? Yeah, things were wonky. Which was why I hadn't let her out of my sight except for a few bathroom breaks in the last six hours. She might have thought she'd left me behind at that damn camp, but I'd been shadowing her ass the whole fucking time.

I supposed that I could have stayed hidden all night, staying out of her way and letting her calm down, but that just wouldn't be my style.

Wren's purple duffle smacked the ground, her green-gold eyes flaring with barely contained rage. I'd ruined her little storm-out and infiltrated her new home. What she didn't realize was—if this place was suitable—it would be our home, our den. We would be here together.

But only if she was safe.

Wren's whole body vibrated like a new pup's, ready to break free of her skin at any moment. But Wren wasn't a wolf. Wolves—like all shifters—had to be born. There was no such thing as turning into one, and I'd never heard of a witch—or anyone else for that matter—taking on the abilities of their mate.

Then again, how would I know? There hadn't

been a wolf to mate outside the species in so long, I doubted anyone knew anymore.

A snarl once again ripped up Wren's throat, full of wolf challenge. Instead of letting it go this time, I met her challenge with one of my own, sliding from her sheets and stalking across the room to get in her space.

Her eyes popped wide at my own snarl—mine a fair sight louder, deeper, and full of every bit of Alpha power. A power I had a sneaking suspicion she was drawing on like I so often did with my wolf.

"See, beautiful, what we have here is a failure to communicate. I need you to listen to me without going off half-cocked. The only way we're going to be able to have a civil conversation is if you get out some of that rage."

I snagged my shirt and pants, donning them without breaking eye contact for more than a few seconds. I'd thought she'd have cooled off by now and we could cuddle in bed and talk it out.

Evidently, I'd been mistaken.

"Let's go."

"Go?" Wren challenged. "Go where? You want to have a knock-down drag-out in the living room?"

Wren hadn't explored her new apartment yet, but while she was getting her bag out of the car, I'd taken a cursory look around. There was a large courtyard just outside the French doors with enough room to let her really let herself rip.

Pointing, I drew her gaze to the doors. "Courtyard, Wren. *Now.*"

When she didn't move, I grabbed her hand and dragged her behind me to the open, ivy-covered space. The courtyard was large, nearly as big a footprint as the house itself, with foliage coating the back walls and along with the stone steps leading down from the street level.

At the center was a trio of concentric circles, most likely used in spell work. Like most homes on this side of town, it was retrofitted to include the arcane and hide it from prying eyes. The wards around this property pressed in on me like a physical thing, which was why I was still considering this being a good place for us.

Letting Wren's hand go, I strode away, leaving a fair bit of space between us before turning. "You learned enough in hand-to-hand combat training to do damage should you need to. I'll promise not to shift, if you promise to get your head in the game and take this seriously."

Plus, I needed to know just how much about Wren had changed in only twenty-four hours. The first time we came together, my bite hadn't done near as much as it was doing now. Maybe because she'd put on a null ward right after the first bite. Maybe because she hadn't known what she'd been agreeing to.

But now?

That bite had taken and then some.

Wren held her hands wide, not bothering to get into a fighting stance. "Why are we doing this? I get the whole 'getting out aggression' bullshit, but really? I'm not a wolf, Nico. And fist fighting my boyfriend in the backyard seems a little more toxic than I'm willing to go."

I am not her boyfriend. I'm her mate—her husband.

This time, I let my wolf shine out of my eyes as a growl rumbled from my chest. "You're mated to a wolf, Wren. Fighting out aggression is what we do. In our race it's healthy. Do you think you're going to hurt me, little bird?"

Wren's eyes narrowed, the green-gold orbs shining like diamonds even in the bright sunlight.

"Come on, then," I taunted, practically begging her to attack. "Show me what little birds can do."

In a flash of red hair, she'd come at me, but not where I'd expected her to. Most people usually came from the front or the back. Wren? She dodged to the left before coming at me from the side, her heel aimed right for my hip. It was a smart move, and as fast as she was moving, it would take out just about anyone—even another wolf. Too bad she was dealing with an Alpha.

I spun right as she extended the kick, making her stumble until I caught her by the back of the shirt, keeping her gorgeous face from meeting the pavement. Granted, I also spanked her luscious ass in the process, but that was neither here nor there.

"Good strategy, Bird. Smart. Try again."

Another snarl ripped up her throat as she turned on me, but instead of attacking as most would do when riled, she flitted away and back, nearly circling me before I had a chance to react. Just like a wolf would, she attacked just outside of my peripheral vision.

She was getting faster, but still, she wasn't fast enough.

Catching the fist she had aimed at my temple, I twisted us both, wrapping her arm around her middle. I'd planned on kissing her neck just so she could see how quickly I could bite her, but I hadn't planned on Wren outsmarting me. Instead of just standing there, she tossed her head back, catching me in the eye.

My grip loosened, and the little minx didn't waste a second. A moment later she'd swept my feet out from under me, and I was on my ass on the cobblestones. Her fist rocketed toward my sternum, but I rolled out of the way before it could land. Up and on my feet again, I watched as her fist powered through solid rock without her even flinching.

"Look at you, little bird," I taunted, loving how my flannel clung to her skin in the too-hot Savannah sunshine. "Look how strong you are. How fucking sexy."

She ripped at the fabric, pulling it from her shoulders with a strength she shouldn't have but turned me the fuck on all the same. Wren hadn't even broken the skin of her knuckles, and if my healing, my strength, my speed was being shared with her, fuck if I was going to complain.

"Fuck you, Nico," she growled, my compliments raising her ire.

"Sure, but later. We're busy." Then, instead of her waiting, I struck, attacking from her right side, my fangs and claws at the ready.

But it didn't catch my woman off guard. No, she caught me by the wrist and used my own momentum against me, flipping me over her hip just like I'd shown the student in her combat class. She expected me to go down, readying an elbow to strike, but midair, I snagged her other wrist, pulling her with me.

The pair of us landed on the stone—her on top of me—surprising my little mate.

She scrambled to her feet, ready to attack again, even though she'd had the wind knocked out of her.

"You're just playing with me," she hissed before coming at me from the side again. "Stop playing with me. It's bad enough you're stuck with me. Can't you ju—"

I caught her fist, holding it in my hand instead of letting her go. "*Stuck* with you? Who the fuck said I was *stuck* with you?"

She ripped her fist out of my hold, leveling me with a look so fierce it was as if she was touching my soul. "*You* did. You don't get to choose your mate, Nico. You got stuck with me. I was thinking about it on the drive down here. No one in your pack is going to want me there. Hell, you probably don't want me th—"

"That's enough," I growled, cutting her off as I crowded into her space. "I swear to everything holy, the next time I see your father, I'm ripping him limb from fucking limb. Him and anyone else who put that voice in your head that tells you you're not good enough. Not a damn one of them see what I do."

Wren's eyes misted over, the glowing green-gold dulling a bit. "What you see is blinded by sex and a mate bond." She shook her head, her gaze drifting off so she didn't have to look me in the eye. "You didn't even like me a week ago."

She didn't know just how wrong she was.

Cupping her chin in my hand, I walked her backward to the closest wall. "When are you going to get it? Huh? I was obsessed with you long before that bite took. Couldn't get you out of my head. Not a single waking minute of peace. Because if I wasn't thinking about your scent or your curves or the way I wanted you underneath me, it was just how fucking astounding you were."

"Is that a euphemism for stupid?"

My hand fisted in her hair, tilting her head back so she had to look at me. "You know it isn't. You know damn well that I have never—not once— thought you were stupid. A pain in my ass, maybe, but never stupid. Who told you that?"

"Nobody," she lied, not bothering to hide it. Her grandmother had called her stupid right in front of me, and what had I done about it?

Nothing, that's what. What I wouldn't give to go back in time and toss Eloise Bannister out on her ass.

"Do you know why I followed you that night at the bar?"

She rolled her eyes. "Mate bond bullshit, I'm guessing."

I pulled her closer—probably rougher than I

should have—but I needed her attention. "No, mate bonds don't work like that. I wouldn't have been called to you until I turned thirty. But something about you made me follow your ass like a little puppy. I needed to figure you out. I needed to know why you were in that apothecary, needed to know why you'd risk yourself that way."

"I didn—"

"I'm not done," I barked, cutting her off. "You risked your life and your freedom to help your friend's mother. Then—shoved into a situation that your family could have *easily* gotten you out of—you stuck it out. You sacrificed your feet for fuck's sake, getting every single student off that mountain. You made sure no one forgot about Fiona. Everything you do is a testament to how lucky I am to have had the universe choose you for me."

I shook my head. "I'm not *stuck* with you. Because I was already half in love with you before that mate call ever came."

Wren didn't take that news like I'd thought she would. No, she looked at me like I was a little crazy. Maybe I was, but I'd be getting it through her thick skull at some point, and I didn't care what I needed to do to make that happen.

"Now, as much as I'd like to strip you naked and spank your ass for trying to leave me behind before fucking you until you finally grasp my point of view, I'm going to need you to maybe consider that the people who have put you down your entire life aren't the best people to judge your character. After that, I'm going to need you to get on board with the fact that if we don't go to the pack house—just to visit, calm down—then my crazy, loud, obnoxiously loving family will indeed break down your door and welcome you to the family, anyway."

Wren appeared positively distressed at the thought of my family railroading into her house.

"Plus, there's that whole 'displaying wolf characteristics while not a wolf' thing. That likely needs to get addressed ASAP—preferably *before* you go into work at ABI headquarters."

Her face paled as her fingers held onto me for dear life.

"So, to recap: I'm not stuck with you, you're not stupid, and yes, while our relationship is unconventional and rare, it is not fake, because of a mate bond, or whatever other bullshit you have in your head."

"You told your parents about me?" she asked on a whisper, her eyes shining with hopeful tears.

Chuckling, I pulled her in, kissing her forehead. "Out of all the shit I just said, that's what you're worried about?"

Not bothering to look at me, she nodded her head against my shoulder.

"For clarity's sake, I was not the one to tell my mother. Wyatt beat me to the punch about a week before we were actually mated. But I walked in there with your scent all over me, which is pretty much the same thing."

"A week?"

Sighing, I pulled her back to the apartment. "It was after the bar incident. And Wyatt has a big mouth. Now, if I know my family—and I do—we have less than an hour before someone will come knocking on your door. This house is nice and all, but I doubt everyone can fit in it."

Wren surveyed her place like she was trying to imagine roughly fifty of my relatives crammed inside. Sure, the apartment was small, but the space had enough character to make up for it. Then she bit her lip as her gaze snagged on her purple duffle.

"I... I don't have anything nice enough to wear to meet your family, Nico."

Wren was wearing a black tank over black leggings, her red hair piled on her head, and because she'd been wearing my flannel all day, she was coated in my scent. She looked absolutely beautiful, and not a single person would care what she was wearing.

Given that she was on the outs with her family—none of them would even bat an eye.

Plus, formal and Acosta had never really been synonymous.

"You are fucking stunning, but there is one thing..."

"Wha—"

Before she could react, I was rubbing my jaw against hers, scent marking her for the whole of my family—and Savannah itself. I kissed the silvery crescent scar on her shoulder, trailing them up before I nipped the lobe of her ear.

Instantly, her scent changed from worry to desire, which was the intended effect.

"There. Now you're ready."

I just hoped I was.

CHAPTER EIGHT

WREN

I f there was ever a time for a sinkhole to pop up and swallow me alive, now was the time. Sitting in the front seat of Nico's truck, I held onto the Lulu's box for dear life as I tried to make myself open the vehicle's door.

There was absolutely no way on this planet or any other that I'd go to meet Nico's mom without at least a treat of some kind. I hesitated going to Lulu's because it was a chocolate bar, but Nico assured me shifters—even wolf ones—were not allergic to chocolate. In fact, it was one of his mother's favorites.

"She's going to love you, Wren," Nico said for the

fifth time since we'd parked, but I could not for the life of me unbuckle my seatbelt.

Before I knew it, the truck was off, and he was rounding the hood, opening my door long before I was ready. I mean, I was in leggings, for fuck's sake. *Leggings.* No hate to the most comfortable form of attire in the universe, but *leggings?*

I needed to be in a sundress with my hair done and enough foundation on to cover my sins, not in workout gear covered in flop sweat because I was meeting Nico's mom in a messy bun.

If my mother could see me now.

Then again, Nico's mama hated mine with a fiery passion—or so I'd heard—so maybe it wouldn't be so bad? The enemy of my enemy and all that?

Oh, who was I kidding? A bunch of sweets weren't going to make up for the fact that Catia Acosta absolutely, positively did not like my family. Not one bit.

"Come on, beautiful. I promise that no one will make you feel unwanted." He shot a look over his shoulder, almost like he was glaring at a window and then turned back to me. "Because if they do, I will tear out their spleen and shove it down their throat."

Swallowing hard, I held out a hand and let Nico pull me from the safety of the truck. "That was graphic."

Then again, I had watched him rip out Girard's throat, so it wasn't too far of a stretch.

"But honest," he replied, guiding me by the shoulders toward the carved front door with a distinct wolf baying at the moon etched into the wood.

The Acosta estate was a no-shit manor house straight out of *Architecture Digest* or something. Spanning two city blocks and butted right up to Forsyth Park, the sprawling home seemed so large and yet almost... warm? The Bannister family home was beyond cold. Sure, it had warm colors and pretty décor, but the life of the place was gone. This house —even as pretty and enormous as it was, already had so much life in it.

And I was still outside.

Instead of knocking, Nico opened the door and waltzed right on in like he owned the place, an act that sent me into a world of wonder and scandalized me all at the same time. I couldn't imagine just walking into my parents' house right now, and even when I lived there, it was more of a "sneak in and pray no one noticed I was home" kind of a situation.

"Nicholas," a woman breathed, descending the stairs like our coming was a surprise. She appeared barely older than Nico did, nary a line or wrinkle to show for what had to be centuries worth of years under her belt. Her glossy black hair was piled on her head into an elegant but messy bun—far classier than mine.

Dressed casually in jeans, a slouchy T-shirt and flats, the woman seemed so put together and so down to earth all at the same time. The signature of power coming off her was strong—strong enough that I hoped this was his mother, or else I was going to run screaming from the house.

Nico was enveloped in a bone-cracking hug, his mother's face the picture of joy at having her boy under her roof.

"Hi, Mom," he said, squeezing her back, a softness to his expression one I hadn't seen before. It was as if several layers had been lifted from him, easing an ache of worry somehow. "There's someone I want you to meet."

Oh, boy. Here we go.

"Mom, this is Wren Bannister, my mate," he said with a sort of pride that made my heart hurt and melt all at the same time. He was so proud of me—of us—and damn if I was going to disappoint him. "Wren, this is Catia Acosta, my mom."

Pasting a smile on my face, I brandished the Lulu's box like it could save me from impending doom. "So happy to meet you, Mrs. Acosta. Nico said you liked Lulu's. Sorry it's no—"

"Lulu's," she exclaimed, clapping like a little kid who just got a treat. "My favorite." But less than a second later, Catia had snatched the box out of my hand, passed it to Nico, and gave me my own bone-crushing hug full of wolf strength. "Oh, my goodness. I'm so happy to meet you. Nicholas has talked my ear off about you. How you did on your final exam and saving your cabin mate. What you must have gone through."

I would have replied, but Catia was cutting off all my air.

"And you brought me my favorite treats when you have gone through so much." Then she let me go, gripping my shoulders and inspecting me like Alice would while I sucked in a breath. "You need a good home-cooked meal and some wine. Yes?"

Wolf culture was brand new to me, but Southern culture dictated that if someone offered you a meal, you damn well took it, or else. "Oh, I wouldn't want to impose."

Nico's mom gave me a single raised eyebrow. "Sweetheart, I can hear your stomach growling." She directed her gaze at Nico. "And I instructed all your brothers and sisters and every pack member that they are to treat your mate with the utmost respect, or else they will eat their own spleen. That is what you wanted to ask, yes?"

She'd totally heard us in the truck.

Note to self: do not mutter anything under your breath at all—ever—around a wolf.

"Yes, Mom," Nico huffed. "Maybe also tell them to dial the crazy back just a little? I don't want to scare her off too early. We at least have to wait for her to meet Theo before this whole thing goes tits up and she runs screaming from the house."

Catia stopped dead in the hallway to fit her hand on her hip and stare her son down. "Nicholas Vincente Acosta, your brother is—"

But Nico was immune to her stare, smiling widely as he captured me under his arm again. "A wildly unhappy pain in my ass. That's not going to change anytime soon. He may be your firstborn, but he's also the reason Lara's husband refuses to sit too close to Dad, and Gustavo's wife nearly has a heart attack every time he gets too close to one of her pups. But sure," he remarked, walking us deeper into the house toward what I figured was a kitchen, "he's the picture of sweetness and light."

Oh, dear. I hadn't quite gotten the tea on Nico's family yet—probably so he wouldn't scare me any more than I already was—but *damn.* I sort of wished I had some popcorn. Honestly, Nico's brother sounded a bit like my aunt Judith... only a little less deadly.

"Don't worry," he rumbled in my ear. "I'll keep you safe."

Of that I had no doubt.

"Really, Nico. Airing out family drama so soon?" another female voice called from behind us. A young woman skipped down the stairs, her dark, wavy hair bouncing with her. Like me, she was in leggings and a top, but hers was slouchy and cute, hanging off one shoulder like she hadn't a care in the world. Devious green eyes sparked with mirth as she got closer. "You should at least let her sit down at the table with some wine in her before she gets all the gory details."

As soon as she caught up with us, she enveloped me in a hug. "Hi, Wren. I'm Mariella, the youngest. You can call me Mari." She let me go and hooked an arm over my shoulder, pulling me from Nico and guiding me to a door. "Has Nico given you the family spiel yet?"

I shook my head as we shoved through to a robust, unpopulated kitchen where the rumble of about a zillion voices filled the air from what I could only assume was the dining room on the other side. There was a fully closed door in between that room and this one, and still, it was as if there was nothing. Eyes wide, I met Mari's gaze as I stuttered us both to a stop.

"Yeah," she said, nodding, "they're loud and

you're going to forget everyone's names—even mine. We decided just the immediate family for the first meeting, so we wouldn't make you run for the hills and leave Nico all heartbroken."

They'd planned this? Shit, Nico wasn't lying. They really would have been to my house in an hour if we hadn't shown up.

Then again, if they showed up at my house, I at least would have had Fiona and Hannah and Malia as backup.

Mari dragged me by the hand to the next room, the voices only growing louder until the group at large noticed us standing in the doorway. Then you could have heard a pin drop. The dining room was probably the biggest room in the house—that I'd seen so far—and it was maybe half full of a boatload of people. Seriously, the number of people here could probably fill a large vessel.

"So, there's Theo, the oldest," Mari said, pointing at the surly man with shoulder-length black hair at the end of the table that everyone seemed to give a wide berth. "Then Mateo, Gustavo and his wife, Zola, Lara and her husband, Logan, Dayana, the twins, Francisco and Ella, Santiago, Nico, then me, of course. Personally, I figure ten kids is too much, but Mom kept popping out babies until she got a grandkid to ease the baby ache, so here we are."

Sweet mother of all that is holy. I really hoped no one in their right mind expected me to start popping out babies anytime soon. I was lucky I was even here and semi-not running for the hills at the mate talk. I'd never been so happy to have an IUD in my freaking life.

"Everyone, this is Wren, Nico's mate."

Wide-eyed, I gave everyone a little wave.

No one seemed shocked or appalled that I was here or ready to kick me out because I was a witch. Sure, Nico had threatened spleen removal, but still.

Each of Nico's siblings got up and gave me a hug —well, all except Theo who stayed at the far end of the table like he wanted no part of this. Honestly, I didn't mind. Knowing who liked me and who didn't was good information to have. At least he was upfront about it.

Mari whispered to one of her other sisters—yes, I'd already forgotten everyone's name at this point. "She brought Mom Lulu's and didn't get all dressed up to meet us like she was going to some garden party. I like her already."

Smiling, I leaned over. "I totally would have dressed like I was going to a garden party, but I told my family to kick rocks yesterday and don't have access to my clothes. Just saying." I waved at my outfit like a gameshow host. "This is accidental."

Mari and her sister snickered, the latter snorting into her wine. "Fair enough. You can stay, but leggings fit in a lot more than dresses do. Have you ever ran at wolf-speed in heels? No thank you."

I blinked at her, wondering if I should say this next bit out loud. "Considering I'm not a wolf, no, but I get your point."

I mean, I had just run barefoot in the snow. It wasn't the same, but I got it.

Mari's sister frowned. "Wait, what?"

Yeah, I'd caught Mari leaving off the Bannister name on that introduction, too, but I figured everyone was going to find out, anyway, so...

"But the bite took," she said, pointing to the very large, totally unmistakable mating mark on my shoulder. "And your eyes are all glowy like a happy pup, and—"

"Her last name is Bannister, Dayana," Theo growled from behind his sister, staring at me like I was a particularly troublesome stain on his favorite shirt. "She's a witch. Can't you smell it on her under Nico's stink?"

When exactly he'd moseyed on over here, I didn't know, but his reception was awfully frosty.

Dayana, to her credit, didn't seem appalled per se, just confused. And what did *eau de witch* smell like exactly? And Nico didn't stink. He smelled like lust and man and... I shook myself as I attempted to not drool in front of Nico's family.

"Guilty," I said, shrugging. I couldn't help I was a witch any more than Nico could help that I was his mate. Speaking of... Searching through the sea of people, I finally located the man in question on the opposite side of the room, cornered by two brothers and a very pregnant sister.

And this is where they tell him he's crazy and to toss me off a cliff or something. Fabulous.

Nico met my gaze, seeming to feel it across the room. His eyes glowed with his wolf as a slow, seductive smile spread over his lips. Okay, so maybe I was overreacting.

"Don't you care that you're hurting his chances of becoming Alpha one day?" Theo demanded, spearing me with a glare. "Or that you're polluting a sacred wolf line that hasn't seen a mating outside the species in four centuries?"

Mari and Dayana smacked their brother—one in the chest and the other upside the head. "Shut up, Theo. Or I'll tell Nico and he can kick your ass from here to Atlanta. When was the last time you bested him in a fight again?"

I bit my lip so I didn't start laughing outright. Plus, I had a feeling if Nico cared about any of the "Alpha coming into power" bullshit, he probably wouldn't have mated me without explaining the details. But that was neither here nor there. And I sure as shit wasn't going to bring the whole "marriage without consent" issue up in this house. Nico and I needed to be a united front, and honestly, I was starting to care less and less.

Tilting my head, I studied Theo who seemed to be doing his level best to make me feel unwanted. Too bad for him I grew up a Bannister outcast. Sure, Theo could probably tear me limb from limb, but his intimidation game was weak.

I'm not stuck with you. Because I was already half in love with you before that mate call ever came.

It was tough to be mad at the man when he said shit like that, and Nico's words were the balm to my nerves that I so needed right that second.

Raising my eyebrows, I held in a snicker. "Sorry, my dude," I said, patting his shoulder. "I'm an outcast in my own family. If you're trying to intimidate me, you're going to need to step up your game. My aunt Judith is scarier than you without lifting a finger. Good try, though."

Truth be told, Aunt Judith could likely raise a single eyebrow and kill someone, so that wasn't as much of an insult as he probably thought it was.

Dayana and Mari both busted out laughing. Like, hanging off each other, almost spilling their wine, about to collapse from the sheer hilarity, laughing. Theo, to his credit, appeared to take it in stride, staring at his sisters like they were complete loons.

I loved them all already—even Theo, who seemed to like me just a little bit now that I'd dished some of his own back at him.

"Honestly, Theo," Catia said, handing me a glass of red wine as big as my head. "Already? At least let the girl get something in her belly before you start on your nonsense. Come on, Wren. Let me fix you a plate before these heathens eat it all."

Dutifully, I followed her, sitting where she told me, and placing the napkin on my lap like a good Southern woman. She dished up a mound of food on my plate, and I let her. Based on the heaps of food covering every available surface, this wasn't a family of dainty eaters.

"Are we waiting on Dad?" one of the brothers asked as the majority of the Acosta family began taking their seats.

See? Theo wasn't who I was scared of. *Theo* was barely a blip, even as he plopped onto his chair right across from me. More than likely, he thought he was protecting his little brother. I was really scared of Nico's father—*and Alpha*. He could disown his son, or kill me on the spot, or... Really, the possibilities were endless, but all of them ended with bloodshed and despair.

And yes, every single scenario ran through my head so much I was cataloging the exits even as I eyed the lemon tarts across the table.

"No," Catia breathed, waving her hand as she rounded the table. "He had to take care of a few things, but he will be in shortly. Fix your plates and dig in, kids."

I hadn't noticed staff anywhere but there was no way Catia cooked this all herself—or if she did, she was *Wonder Woman*. Four baskets of biscuits dotted the impossibly long table in between platters of sliced tri-tip, mashed potatoes, mac and cheese, chicken fried steak, collard greens, and pretty much any other comfort food I could possibly imagine. On my plate was a sample of a little of everything—my personal favorite thing to do at any cookout ever—plus a little plate on the side with three rolls and my own little dish of butter.

Hesitating, I watched and waited, my shoulders only relaxing once Nico took the chair to my left in between me and the open seat at the head of the table. Across from me was Theo and beside him— and closest to the head seat—was Catia, finally sitting down now that all her children were settled.

Nico pressed a kiss to my temple, threading his

fingers through mine as he sat, before picking up his fork with his left hand and digging in. For the first time since we got here, I took a full breath. Nico swallowed his bite and then leaned over. Everyone was talking, bantering back and forth as they filled their plates, and somehow it felt like we were alone in this sea of people.

"Eat, little bird," he whispered. "You'll need your strength for later."

Nico's scalding gaze drifted to my lips before falling to my shoulder, his eyes glowing gold as they snagged on my mark.

A shiver worked its way up my spine. I'd need *a lot* of strength for later.

And that happy bubble lasted about forty-five minutes.

Less than an hour of banter and getting to know this crazy loud loving family.

Less than an hour to fall in love with every single one of them.

Less than an hour to get a glimpse of how families should be—how mine would have been if they would have loved me like they were supposed to.

That bubble lasted right up until a tall, raven-haired man shoved through the dining room doors with an elderly woman at his side, his decidedly unfriendly gaze trained right on me.

This was Nico's father—I knew it without a doubt. And he didn't like me one bit.

Yep. I was doomed.

CHAPTER NINE

NICO

The mashed potatoes in my mouth turned to lead as my father strode into the room, his spine straight, his shoulders tight, his scent *off*. But it wasn't exactly my father that had my gut churning, it was the ancient woman trailing after him that did it.

Though she stood tall, Diana Silva was a thousand if she was a day, her silver hair cascading down her back in a waterfall. Her face was lined with the passing of time, her eyes a milky, sightless blue that had been that way as long as anyone could remember. And if the rumors were true, she was the last surviving non-wolf member of our pack. Sure, there had been some non-wolves mated after her, but most of them had died out in the vampire wars that made Savannah what it was today.

The conversations hushed, dying out once people recognized the elder in the room, but Wren? She sat stock-still, not breaking eye contact with my father as she finished chewing her bite and swallowing. Then she dotted her lips with her napkin and gently laid the fabric on the table, ready to get up if necessary.

Ready to run.

She didn't freeze exactly, but she moved with a deliberate slowness that had me thinking she was trying not to look like prey.

To anyone else, Wren's expression and rigid posture might look like a challenge, but I saw it for the starch upbringing and Southern lady etiquette it was. Wren was giving him her unwavering attention, not backing down an inch. What she was also doing was looking an awful lot like an Alpha herself. Even though fear, alarm, and a fair bit of sorrow filled our connection, she didn't show it, I couldn't scent it.

Then again, displaying weakness in the Bannister house would likely get her in a world of hurt. Wren was used to not looking like prey. It was probably the only way she survived as long as she had.

Standing, I almost winced at the sound of my chair scraping against the hardwood floor. Almost.

That sound had every eye on me and off Wren, allowing her to breathe a little.

"Dad, Diana, I would like you to meet my mate, Wren Bannister. Wren, this is my father, Tomás and my great-grandmother, Diana."

Wren inclined her head, not breaking eye contact with my father, even long enough to blink. "I'm pleased to meet you both."

My father lifted a single eyebrow, one of his signature stoic expressions that could mean anything from pleased, to enraged, to ready to rip someone limb from limb.

He tipped up his chin in acknowledgment. "It's time we had a conversation, son. Bring your bride."

Rage slammed through the connection, Wren's eyes glowing with my wolf. "Is this a last meal kind of a situation? Because Catia made these gorgeous lemon tarts, and if this is going to be my last meal, I'd like to sample them before I go."

The sheer amount of sass in Wren's voice had me aching to spank her ass and buy her a damn pony all at the same time. The only person on Earth who talked to my father that way was my mom. Most people got their throats torn out for far less.

The room froze—myself included—as I prayed that this would not be the day I'd have to challenge my dad. The place was so silent, you could hear a pin drop. Hell, no one even breathed until Theo, of all people, burst out laughing. I didn't think I'd heard my brother laugh in years—decades even—and Wren had not only sassed him and my dad on the same day but made his perpetually grumpy ass laugh.

There were reasons Theo didn't smile often. Hell, if I'd been searching for my mate for going on a century, only to have her die mere weeks from me finding her, I'd be a solid pain in the ass, too.

Both my parents, all my siblings, and their spouses stared from Wren to Theo as my eldest brother wiped tears from his eyes. Hell, if he had fallen out of his chair I wouldn't have been surprised.

"Lemon tarts," Theo wheezed. "Okay, she can stay. If anything, it'll up the entertainment value of this place."

The corner of my father's lips turned up ever so slightly as he squeezed Theo's shoulder. No one had Theo's approval. Not Zola, Gustavo's wife, or Logan, Lara's husband. Theo didn't think they were good enough, didn't care enough, didn't love our siblings enough.

But Wren did.

"Leave the tart. You'll come back for it."

I hadn't expected Wren to get Theo's approval— in fact, I assumed she wouldn't. Especially with her being a witch. I just hoped my father followed Theo just this once.

Wren nodded, standing with me and we marched behind my dad and Diana toward one of three soundproof meeting rooms. Of all the places to take us, I sort of wished he'd have picked something a little more open. I trusted my father. I did, but if he'd decided on doing something, he wouldn't always listen to reason. And if he decided Wren and I couldn't be, well, it was going to be a challenge.

I hadn't lied to Wren when I said everyone would love her. But my father could love someone and know in his whole heart and soul that they had to go all at the same time. He made the hard decisions— the ones no one wanted to make.

I just wouldn't let him make this one.

My father's downstairs study boasted a large library and hidden bar behind a speakeasy-type sliding bookshelf.

"Would either of you like a drink?" he asked, leading Diana to one of the leather wingbacks situated in front of his sprawling desk before heading for the hidden bar.

But his chivalrous air didn't fool me one bit. If Dad brought Diana here, there was something wrong, and him easing into it wouldn't help a damn thing.

"None for me, thank you," Wren replied from behind me when I'd let the silence stretch on for far too long.

"Tomás tells me you are a witch like me," Diana said, holding out her wrinkled hand for Wren to take. "Come here, child. Let me look at you."

Diana didn't mean "look" like anyone else would —tough to do considering she was blind—she meant *look*. She wanted to see into Wren and advise my father like she'd done so many times before.

Wren made to move, but I caught her by the waist and tucked her behind me. My wolf was screaming at me that this place was not safe, his voice so loud after being absent for so long. But why had he been gone? Was Wren drawing on me *and* him? Was my power fading with the mate bond?

"You can see her just fine from here."

Don't you touch her. No one touches her.

Diana's milky blue eyes landed on me, making me feel about five years old and about four feet shorter. "You shield her too much, boy. Can't you see how powerful she is? How strong? What do you have to fear from family, Nicholas?"

Her words tasted like dirt in my mouth, like lies and danger and more. "That depends on what your intentions are. I could have a lot to fear if you plan on hurting her."

My father stalked to his desk, his cut crystal glass hitting the desktop hard enough to make me flinch. I backed us up a step, ready to run if I had to. It wouldn't be fast enough—I had never been faster than my father—but damn if I wouldn't try.

I might be the next Alpha, but I wasn't ready to take him on.

Not yet.

"No one is going to take your mate from you, Nicholas. Diana just needs to inspect your bond. Your mother told me about how she has been displaying some odd wolf behavior—especially for a witch—and we need to know if the bond was formed appropriately. Though, considering how protective you are, I'd say you have nothing to worry about."

Wren squeezed my arm reassuringly before sliding out of my hold and heading toward Diana. It took everything I had in me not to catch her by the middle and rip her out of this room. She took the seat next to the ancient witch and across from my father, offering Diana her hand.

"Pleasure to meet you, again," Wren said, before her fingers were snatched up in Diana's palm, the elder witch's eyes glowing with a power I'd hardly ever seen before.

"You have been through much, child," Diana began, her voice a breathy whisper. "A life of hardship.

And your family has taken much from you, leeched your light and your power for their own gain. But you found a new family—one that saved you from despair. One that you fought for—both as a child and now."

Diana's head cocked to the side, those sightless, glowing eyes trained right on me as a look of solid disapproval flowed over her features. "Your mate found you before the calling—rare indeed—drawn to you as if guided by Fate, and the bond formed— unconventional as it is. But *Nicholas.* You did not ask? I'm disappointed in you."

That stung. "There was a misunderstanding. Questions were asked, but I wasn't clear. I incorrectly made an ass—"

"You know what assuming does, son," my father broke in. "How can you lead if you do not first require clarity?"

It wasn't like I could tell my father that I was too busy thinking with my dick at the time to gain any clarity whatsoever. I wanted to ask him how clear he felt once the moon hit him on his thirtieth birthday, how much say he had in what he did and said. I wanted to ask if at any point if he'd been presented with his mate—one he was already in love with—if he would have thought it through.

I didn't think anything through—nor had I been

capable—but I wouldn't change anything. Especially if it meant not making Wren mine.

Smartly, all I said was a bland, "So noted."

Truth be told, the only person who could judge me right now was Wren, and if that ghost of a smile on her face told me anything, it was that she was thinking of the exact moment I mated her, the very second my teeth broke her skin and marked her for me.

"Your bond is strong—stronger than I've ever seen—but it draws on you both. Your family draws on you, child," Diana whispered, her eyes widening as she readjusted her grip on Wren. "They are stealing what is rightfully yours, leeching your power to amplify their spells. Burdening you to a half-life. A cursed life. There is a curse upon you, child, put there by your family."

Wren ripped her hand out of Diana's grasp, knocking over the chair as she scrambled away.

"You're lying. They may not like me, but they wouldn't curse me." She shook her head. "I'm their blood, their family. No one would do that to family—not even mine."

But she was wrong, wasn't she? Time and time again her family had put her down, called her names, or forgot she even existed. In a blink, Wren was in my arms, my feet carrying me to her without my brain ever telling them to.

"They wouldn't, Nico. No one could do that to family," she repeated, her eyes welling.

"They could, beautiful. Don't lie to yourself, painting them as something better than they are. There's something up, Wren, and we need to get to the bottom of it."

Who knew if we even could, but I wanted her to be free of them—free of their weight on her shoulders. Diana and my father could fix it. Couldn't they?

"But *cursed*? Why? What purpose does that serve, other than me being a pain in their assess for twenty-four years? It makes no sense."

Diana chuckled. "Many things that are done for power make no sense. Why harm a child? Why make a deal? Why trade with someone you shouldn't? Power, child. Power. And they steal from you even now. You can feel it, can't you? The doubt, the worry, the fatigue." Diana turned to my father. "The Bannister matriarch steals from not just Wren, but Nicholas as well. Stealing Acosta power, shifter power. Power she should. Not. Have."

If I had linked myself to Wren and Wren drew on me, then... *Fuck.*

"Son of a bitch," I growled, turning toward the

door. The urge for blood was so strong, I almost couldn't think straight.

I really should have gutted that bitch when I had the chance. Fuck throwing her out on her ass, I should have sliced my claws into her flesh and tore her the fuck apart. I was nearly out of the room before Wren caught my clawed hand, her soft touch stopping me in my tracks.

"We have to break her curse, free her from her family's shackles," Diana advised my father, her eyes glowing bright as if she was seeing far into the future.

"Yes," Wren breathed, skirting around me. "*Please.*"

"That is if you want her to stay in the family," Diana mused, sitting back in her chair. "Killing her would be far simpler. The other two options spill far too much blood."

Wren stumbled back a step before she was behind me, the growl ripping up my throat a warning. My father steepled his fingers, surveying us with a calculating expression I had never seen on his face.

"I'm warning you both," I snarled, backing toward the door. "Either of you touch her, and I'll rip your throats out myself. I don't give a fuck if you are family. Understand?"

"Wren will need to bleed either way," Diana

murmured, her eyes glowing once more as she stared off into the distance. "Whether Death herself comes for your bride or not is up to the Fates."

And then Wren's hand wasn't in mine anymore. No, she was ripped from me, and by the time I turned around, my brother Theo had a knife to her throat, the blade pressing into the tender skin.

I met Wren's gaze, her eyes wide with the fear that flooded our connection.

Wren was right.

We never should have come here.

CHAPTER TEN

WREN

I wanted to ask why—why put a knife to my throat, why I would need to bleed, why I needed to die—but I knew enough about the arcane world to know that the answer would be murky at best. Especially coming from what had to be a seer. Some called them oracles or psychics, but many witches with the sight were batshit crazy at best and at worst?

They were instigators of more war and strife and drama than you could throw a stick at.

While half of me still wondered if any of this was true—if my family would really curse me—the other half recalled a faint niggle of a memory, tickling my brain from when I had to have been a small child.

Blurry faces surrounding me as I called for my mama. The light of the candles glinting off a knife. Something biting into my flesh as they chanted in a language I didn't know.

A bright orange light.

Pain, so much pain.

Maybe that memory was true, maybe it really happened, or maybe it was a dream. Maybe it was the fevered imaginings of my subconscious, begging for another family not to let me down—to not let the Acostas be anything like the family I was born into.

Whoever held me tightened their grip as they roughly yanked me to the side, the blade at my neck jostling with the motion. Diana's words swirled in my head as the knife's edge bit into my skin, a warm wetness of blood trickling down my neck.

Whether Death herself comes for your bride or not is up to the Fates.

They were going to slit my throat. They were going to kill me.

"Don't move, Wren," Nico warned, his face etched in lines of fear for maybe the first time ever. He didn't think we were going to make it, but damn if he wouldn't fight till the end. "Just stay still, and I'll handle this. Okay?"

131 MAGIC AND MAYHEM

As hopeful as I was that Nico could yank my ass out of these flames, I wanted to flick him. *Stay still.* Did he honestly believe I was going to start some shit with a shifter twice my size and four times my age while he held a knife to my throat?

I was impulsive, yes.

A complete moron? No.

Nodding was off the table, so I settled for a simple "Okay," threading as much strength into my voice as I could muster. Nico's gaze moved from me to the man at my back, a snarl erupting from his throat.

"I'm going to break every bone in your hand for touching her, and when I'm done, I'll rip the heart from your chest and eat it. And there's not a damn thing our father can do to save you from me."

The man clucked his tongue. "You know better than to make promises you can't keep, little brother," Theo rumbled, his grip on my middle tightening as he moved us farther into the room. "You might be an Alpha, but you're not *my* Alpha. There's no way you'd best me—not with your witch in the way."

Theo pressed the knife into my skin more, making me hiss.

"Plus, you've got bigger problems than me."

Before Nico could turn, a black wolf the size of a damn horse tackled him from behind. Instantly, Nico jumped to his animal, and then the two wolves rolled in a tornado of black and gray fur and fangs. But it didn't matter that Nico was the smaller of the two, he was faster, fiercer, and he was out for blood.

And Nico and his brother weren't the only ones causing a ruckus. The study seemed a hell of a lot smaller now filled with the Acosta clan—some in wolf form, some not.

"You can't do this," Dayana screeched at Tomás, slapping papers off her father's desk. "Pack law—"

Santiago yanked his sister away. "Pack law is for the pack. She's not a wol—"

But Dayana was having none of it, her hand morphing from human to wolf so fast Santiago never had a chance to react. Those claws raked across his face, splitting his cheek wide.

"She's his mate, Santi. Wolf or not." Then she pounced, jumping to a beautiful salt-and-pepper wolf before the siblings erupted into a brawl, knocking each other into the bookcase and spilling the books to the ground as the blood sprayed.

The twins, Francisco and Ella were battling it out just outside the study in the hall as Mari and Catia barreled through the door. Mother and daughter split up, Mari coming to me while Nico's mom leapt to her wolf and on top of her husband's desk. The growl that came from her belly had Tomás scrambling backward, and all the while, Diana seemed to pretend she wasn't in the middle of the battle she caused.

Sighing, the ancient woman stood, opening a slouchy leather satchel I hadn't realized she was carrying before now. With a wave of her hand, she knocked Catia off the desk before digging into the bag. She pulled out a mortar and pestle, spell ingredients, and a book bigger than a damn atlas from the bag. Immediately, fear took hold.

No spells. A spell might kill us all.

Then again, I did have a knife to my throat, so I figured death was probably on the table either way. And I would have stayed glued to whatever it was that Diana was doing, except that my focus strayed to the petite woman staring at her brother like she'd never seen him before in her life.

"How could you?" Mari hissed, edging toward us. "After everything you lost, after everything you could have had? How could you take from another this way? How could you want to kill your brother's mate?"

I didn't know what Theo had been through, but a lot of people did a lot of shitty things for absolutely no reason whatsoever—no good ones, anyway.

Maybe Mari had more faith in people than I did,

because the shock seemed too much for her. Her eyes welled with rage-filled tears, and she violently slapped them away. I wanted to tell her to help Nico. I was fine-ish right then, and Nico needed more help than me.

"I'm doing what needs to be done, Mari. And sometimes mates die."

Theo tightened his grip on me, pulling us until our backs were to the far bookcase near Tomás' little bar. Oh, what I wouldn't give to have taken that drink five minutes ago. Maybe then I could relax while I shuffled off this mortal coil. Instead, I was worried more about whatever Diana was cooking up instead of my own skin.

"You should know that spell work backfires around me," I called over the din of snarling wolves and fighting siblings as I watched Diana mix ingredients into her mortar. "It burns buildings down, makes things explode. If you care about this family, I'm going to need you to stop."

The old woman spared me a beatific glance. "I know what I'm doing, child. If you survive, you'll thank me."

Sure I would, and she probably did know what she was doing. And Carmichael Jones knew exactly what he was doing, too. Right up until he blew up his own damn apothecary.

My gaze shifted to Mari. "Get everyone out of here," I ordered, trying to use some of Nico's Alpha tone in my voice so she knew I meant business. "If she's set on doing this, this whole house could burn down. Your family could get hurt."

She squinted, seeming to make a split-second decision and then didn't listen to a fucking word I said. Because instead of running for the hills herself, or oh, I don't know, getting her family away from the ancient timebomb mixing up probable death, she went for the witch herself.

Leaping to her wolf, Mari raced for the old woman, eating up the short distance between them in the blink of an eye. She jumped, dodging the witch's power and attacked from the side. But it didn't matter that Diana was older than Satan himself or that Mari was one of the fastest wolves I'd ever seen.

Mari never even got within an inch of Diana.

All it took was a single glare from the ancient woman, and Mari was tossed across the room as if she was pulled by an invisible string, sailing into a bookcase and landing with a whimper in a pile of books and broken bones.

"Please," I whispered. "You can't let her do that spell—not with everyone here. Theo, please."

Because if what Diana said was true, my family

wasn't just drawing on me. With our bond, they were drawing on Nico. On his Alpha power. On the Acosta line. Drawing on me was bad enough, but Nico, too?

I wanted that curse gone.

I wanted to breathe without worrying if I'd hurt someone else.

I wanted the people around me safe.

I just didn't want everyone in this house to die because an old woman was too damn stubborn to listen to me.

"Shut up," Theo growled, jostling me so that the knife bit into my skin.

"You don't understand," I said, totally *not* shutting up. "Azalea Apothecary burned down because Carmichael did a spell with me in the room. *Please.* I don't care about me. Save your family, Theo."

The knife slipped just a little before it came back stronger, then Theo spun me, shoving me against the wall, the blade just under my chin as he wrapped the other one around my throat and studied my face.

"I can't tell if you're lying or not," he spat, his eyes glowing green with his wolf. "You smell too much like my brother for me to tell. But witches lie all the time. You're no different."

Was I different? Probably not, but I *was* telling the truth.

"Break my leg or something if you don't want me to run, just get Nico out of here," I hissed. "Keep him safe. Get your family out. *Please*."

Theo's grip got tighter. "Tempting. Breaking your leg sounds fun and all, but I'll do as I'm told rather than take your suggestion. Good try, though."

"Bring her here, Theo," Diana called over the din, beckoning us over to her smoking mortar.

Shhhhhiiiiiitttttttt.

I dug in my heels as much as possible, but Theo picked me up by my throat and hauled me to Diana like I weighed less than a freaking feather. At that point, I didn't give a shit that there was a knife at my throat, I kicked Theo as hard as I could in the knee, the bone and cartilage crunching underneath my foot.

His eyes widened as his grip slipped on both me and the knife. He started to fall, and I aimed another kick to his stomach, knocking him away from me as I tried to run. But I wasn't expecting Diana to move as fast as a wolf, or for her to use a taloned hand to pin me to the spot, wrapping around my throat in an unbreakable vise grip.

"You have such fire in you, girl. Such life. And while it would be easier to simply kill you, it would tear this family apart. If you make it to my age, you'll look back on all the people you should have just snuffed out, wondering if you'd done it different, if the Fates would have smiled on you instead."

She leaned closer, eyeing me like she was trying to see inside my soul. "I may be wrong about you—I hope I am. I pray the Fates look kindly on you, that you survive this. Just know that this way—as barbaric as it is—was the least violent option."

My gaze found Nico, his arms pinned behind his back as his brothers and father held him down. His gold eyes glowed, his fangs and talons at the ready but restrained by so many hands, so much power. He wouldn't reach me, couldn't save me.

Then she slammed my back onto Tomás' desk, knocking the air out of me as what felt like invisible chains kept me immobile. Snapping her fingers, Theo's knife flew into her free hand, and in an instant, it raced for my throat. The blade sliced through the flesh so fast I could do nothing to stop her.

Hot blood poured from my neck as I choked, my now-free hands scrabbling for my throat to stop the flow.

And as my sight wavered, the howl of a wolf rang through my ears, its melancholy call breaking my heart as the organ slowed.

Sorry, Nico. I thought we had more time.

But we didn't.

Our time had run out.

CHAPTER ELEVEN

NICO

I'd never felt like a bigger failure in my life than when I watched Theo put a knife to Wren's throat. Never felt weaker than when my family held me down and I met Wren's gaze across that destroyed study. Never more betrayed than when my father used his Alpha power against me, forcing me to bend to his will. Never felt more helpless than when I couldn't stop that woman before she sliced through my mate's throat.

And I had never felt more rage in my life than when I watched Wren try to stop the blood pouring from the wound, her fluttering hands shaking with the tremors of her impending death.

Wren's agony, her fear, her helplessness all combined with my own, forcing a howl from my throat, the sound claiming something I had yet to accept before now. Because there was no going back to the way things were. There was life before Wren and there was life after Wren, and I prayed to everything—every deity, every spirit, every demon and trickster, every single being with more power than I possessed that I could save her.

My howl sent a shockwave through the room, knocking my brothers back, shoving my father away, making my mother whimper as she stood guard over Mariella's still form. Dayana was around here somewhere, fighting alongside me to save Wren. My sisters were breathing, I knew that much, but I couldn't care about any of it.

Because Wren was dying.

Her heart slowed with the blood loss, her skin graying, her breaths shallow, and I wasted no time getting to her, holding her in my arms as our fingers mingled in the blood. Wren's mouth moved as she tried to speak, but Diana had cut so deep, there was no way Wren could talk—hell, it was a wonder she could fucking breathe. Her eyelids drooped, and she struggled to keep them open.

"Baby, please," I pleaded, trying to shake her

awake. "Come on, Bird, stay with me. Please, Wren. Please just stay with me."

I'd thought I'd felt helpless before, but this... this was so much worse.

Heal her. Fuck the consequences. Just heal her.

"I'm gonna fix it, okay? Just stay, beautiful. *Please.*"

Before I could summon my wolf, Diana snatched my bloody hand from Wren's neck, the old woman's grip tighter than even my father's had been.

"No," she hissed, her sightless eyes burning a hole in me. "Not until the curse is broken, boy."

She was keeping me from saving Wren. All this to break a curse I wasn't even sure she had. I didn't feel like I'd been drawn on, and who gave a shit if the Bannisters did it if it meant Wren's death?

"Fuck your curse," I growled, trying to rip my hand from her grasp.

"Here." She slapped a glass bottle filled with black dust in my hand and yanked the stopper from the top.

I recognized the substance right away by the smell. *Black salt.* But black salt was a low-powered way to cross witch circles. It wasn't going to break a curse, and it wasn't going to heal her, and it sure as *shit* wasn't going to put *Humpty Dumpty* back together again.

"Fuck you," I growled, not caring one bit who she was. She wasn't anything to me—not anymore. None of them were.

Diana rolled her eyes before guiding my hand to Wren's wound. "Pour it on the cut and hold on."

Cut? I'd seen near beheadings that were less brutal.

I didn't know why I followed her advice or why I felt a spark of hope in it, but I dumped the whole bottle on Wren's wound and held on just like she told me to. It had two seconds to work before I did whatever it was I had to do to fix this. If it meant giving her what she wanted to get Wren healed, well, then, so fucking be it.

As soon as the granules hit, the blood hissed, bubbling like a goddamn science experiment. On instinct, I pressed my hand against the mounded salt, letting it burn us both with a heat that seared my flesh much like it was Wren's. A convulsion rocked her whole body, Wren's fluttering eyelids flashing open as her mouth widened with a silent scream.

Irises glowing, Wren's chest heaved, trying to suck in a breath that just wasn't hers to have.

"Hold her, boy," Diana insisted, but I didn't understand.

I *was* holding her. I was holding on with all I had.

Then as the charge of magic hit the air, I finally understood.

A shockwave of a spell breaking rocked the entire room, cracking the walls and shaking the earth beneath. What books were still left on the shelves rattled to the ground, the chandelier snapped from its fastenings and shattered on the floor. My family shouted in alarm, but I didn't care about them—not anymore.

And I held on as if Death was coming for Wren and I could fight her off myself.

Hell, I *would* fight her off. She wasn't taking her, not without me.

Wren's body seemed to fold in on itself as her irises dimmed, her breath stuttered along with her heart. Too late. I was going to be too late.

"Now, Nicholas," Diana whispered as the tremors finally quieted. "*Now.* Save your bride."

Sucking in a full breath, I called for my wolf, him coming to me far faster than he had been just moments before. And he gave, he gave all he had to give to Wren.

Because he could.

Because he was now free, the curse's weight no longer pulling at either of us. I hadn't realized it was there until it was gone.

Because she was ours.

Because he loved her as much as I did. And I did love her. More than life and breath and the fucking sun in the goddamn sky. I loved her before the mate call and before the bar. I loved her the moment I dragged her sexy ass out of the burning building, I just hadn't known it.

So he and I gave everything we had. I'd told Wren what seemed like a lifetime ago that she owned all of me, and she did. So if it meant that I'd paste a target on my back, if it meant that my pack might disown me, if it meant she'd live instead of me, well, then I was taking that chance.

The pulse of blood at her throat slowed as her heart picked up speed, thundering in her chest as her breaths restarted. Gently, I pulled my hand away, watching as the skin knitted itself back together. But Wren had been so close to death that the sheer power needed to heal her had taken its toll.

My nose began to bleed, and the coppery tang filled my mouth as darkness crowded the edges of my vision. *Just a little more...*

Wren's eyes flashed open, the glowing green-gold a sight I thought I would never get again. Her gaze finally met mine and she reached up, cupping my jaw like it was precious as she wiped the blood from my upper lip. Frowning, she didn't seem to understand, but still, she gave me my power back and then some. The spark of life—of her power—bloomed between us, flooding our connection, filling me up, letting me breathe again.

It was as if she plugged me into a fucking outlet with as much power as she gave me. And still, I just couldn't let her go, couldn't think about anything but her breathing, her living.

"Nico?" she croaked, trying to sit up, but I held her tighter, cradling her to my chest like someone was going to rip her from me. Hell, they damn near did. "Can we go home now? I don't want to be here anymore."

Staring at my family over her shoulder, I could say without a doubt in my mind that we agreed on that sentiment wholeheartedly.

A hand slapped my arm, and I fought off the urge to snap those fingers off with my teeth. "Get up, son," Diana scolded. "Let me look at her."

A snarl worked its way up my throat as my fangs and claws extended in an instant. "You're not fucking touching her again."

"Let me up," Wren whispered, and I reluctantly let her push herself out of my arms and climb to standing.

She wasn't steady on her feet—who would be after damn near dying?—but she still approached Diana, assessing her with a calculating gleam in her eye. It was the same look she gave Ames in the practical exam right before she shot him until she'd emptied her mag. In a flash, Wren's hand cracked across Diana's face, a red handprint blooming bright on the crone's cheek.

The old woman stumbled, shock written all over her expression as she staggered to the lone upright piece of furniture in the room and half fell into it.

"I appreciate you breaking my curse, but fuck you. Fuck you and everyone who went along with nearly taking me away from him. Fuck you for damn near killing me. Fuck. You. There was another way, and you know it. You just chose not to see it."

Wren's legs wobbled, and I swept her up in my arms, ready and willing to leave this place and never come back. Because how could I call this place a home if she could never feel safe here? How could I be a member of this pack when I couldn't trust the Alpha?

And how could I be a member of this family when so many of my brothers betrayed me?

My father stood in my way, his face bloody, his suit torn to shreds. I'd done a good amount of damage, but it hadn't been enough.

"Son—"

My glare cut him off. "You will give reparations for this. I told my wife that this place was safe—that she could find a family in us—and you made me a liar. You could have trusted us—trusted me—but instead you caused us harm."

My father advanced, but I'd be damned if anyone got to Wren again. "You don't understand. Our options were limited. We had to do something today or else it could have killed you. Sometimes Alphas have to make decisions for the greater good. Please, so—"

"I am not your son. After what you pulled, you don't get to placate me with 'son' ever again." I held Wren closer, tempted to bury my nose in her hair. The problem was, all I could smell was the blood and it just pissed me off. "And as an Alpha, you should have foreseen the ripple this would cause. Instead of talking to me, instead of telling me what needed to be done and allowing me to do it, you had your seer slit my wife's throat while I watched. Fuck you and your greater good."

My gaze drifted to a bloody Theo, a healing Mateo, and the rest of my brothers. They had followed my father without question, and each one of them bending to his will. "This is the Alpha you follow? A man who would have you betray your own brother?"

Slowly, I returned my attention to my father. "You have injured an Alpha's mate, and according to pack law, you *will* make reparations. My mate will decide how much you owe. And you will pay. In blood."

"Tell me—what could I have done different? The only other way to break the curse was to kill every last Bannister witch. Would you have had me do that instead? Or would you prefer I just have killed your mate outright?"

I didn't know the right answer—though, that Bannister murder spree sounded fucking awesome right about now—but it wasn't this.

"Look around you," I growled, the Alpha order strong enough that the man actually did it. "Your mate fought you against this. Your daughters. You caused a rift, ripping your whole family apart. And you still claim that this was the best option. *Look* at what you've done."

My father's face seemed to age before my eyes as it fell. "I just wanted to save you."

"No, you wanted to save the power in our line." That statement didn't feel quite true, but then again, maybe it did. "It wasn't about me. Because had it been about me, you would have treated me like a son and not a subordinate."

"That's not tru—"

I couldn't hear another word—not with Wren's fear and the scent of blood in my nose and the sorrow building up in my chest at what I had just lost. Because it wasn't just almost losing the woman I loved.

It was the betrayal of my brothers—that they wouldn't go against Dad. It was the way they fought our sisters, our mother, all because Dad said so. It was the loss of safety—of family—that hurt the worst.

"I hope you like that Alpha seat. I hope you enjoy that crown. Maybe it'll help you sleep at night, old man."

Dad's eyes widened. "Please, so—*Nicholas*—just listen to me."

But he didn't have his Alpha sway over me anymore, and he knew it.

Wren's grip tightened on my shoulders. It was time to go.

"Almost done, Bird. Almost done," I said, rubbing her back.

Without another word, I went to Mariella who was still whimpering in pain. I set Wren down behind my mother who was still in full wolf form and on red alert. Mom curled around her, guarding my mate with her body. Then I knelt at my sister's side, gripped her ankle, and met my father's eyes as I let my wolf heal my sister.

"How?" Dad breathed, taking a stuttering step toward us until Mom's growl stopped him in his tracks. "This whole time? Why keep it a secret? Wh—"

"It wasn't for you to know."

When Mari was breathing easier, I moved to Mom, easing the cuts in her flesh that her wolf hadn't healed yet. Then while Mom and Mari were protecting Wren, I walked right past my father and went to Dayana, giving him my back in the ultimate sign of disregard.

Still in human form, Dayana was cradling her face to stem the flow of blood from her destroyed eye and cheek. Pulling on my wolf—on the power Wren was lending me—I helped my sister. Instantly, her cuts knitted themselves back together, her eye regenerating and shining with her wolf.

A cold nose bumped me in the cheek, and I turned to find my sister, Ella. Her white pelt stained red, though it wasn't her blood. She whined, nearly begging me to follow her, but I wouldn't. Even though he was her twin, Francisco had sided with Dad.

"No, Ell—"

Ella's wolf dissolved into the mist of her change, revealing my sister's teary eyes. "He changed his mind. Frankie told me to tell you he was sorry, but... I hurt him. Badly. *Please.*"

If there was a fighter that I wanted on my side, it

was Ella. My big sister was one of the fiercest wolves I'd ever met. Had the Alpha gene passed to her, she'd be running her own pack by now, of that I had no doubt.

Gritting my teeth, I shoved out of the study to find Frankie on the stairs, half his guts sitting on the riser beside him.

"Jesus fucking Christ, Ella."

Dad was so worried about losing me, he didn't bother to think how hard some of us would fight to not hurt an innocent—to not lose that bit of humanity that tied us to honor. In doing what he thought he had to, he had now almost killed a son and broken his whole family.

"Heya, Frankie," I whispered, putting a hand on his chest. Shallow breaths and pants of pain pulled at my brother as his dark-brown eyes focused on me. It was bleary, but he did it. No wolf in the world could heal from this—not without help.

"I'm sorry, Nic. Dad said she was hurting you. I-I thought I was helpin—"

His words were cut off by a hiss of pain as I gave him all I could. But this wasn't a shattered leg or a destroyed eyeball. This was major organ damage. The sheer fact that he was still breathing was a miracle. I didn't know if I could put Frankie to rights, and that made me burn up inside.

"Let me help," Wren said, her arm slung over my mother's shoulder. Her face was finally getting its color back, but her jaw was firm, and I knew she wouldn't let me do this on my own.

A moment later, Wren's hand was on my shoulder as she shoved power into me, helping me heal Frankie, when before, I could not.

He'd be scarred, but my big brother wouldn't die, and that was about all I could hope for.

And once he was out of the woods, I stood, grabbing Wren's hand, and directed my feet to the door. If I knew my mother, she would pack up my things and have them sent to me.

Because I wouldn't be coming back here—not until my father was willing to pay the price.

CHAPTER TWELVE

WREN

I'd never been less happy to be right in my entire life. Every few seconds, my fingers found my neck to make sure the wound was no longer there. It got to the point on our twenty-minute drive back to Fiona's house that Nico grabbed my hand, lacing his fingers with mine so I wouldn't keep doing it.

Stuck parking on the street, Nico and I trudged in the front door, looking like we'd just come from battle. Well, we kind of had, but that's beside the point. I'd sort of hoped that no one would notice, but my luck had been shit today, so of course everyone was not only home, but staring at the front door like they were waiting on me.

"What in the high holy hell happened to you?" Fiona damn near screeched as she practically flew down the stairs to Hannah's street-level apartment. "I swear to the Fates, Wolf-boy, you better have a damn good explanation for why my friend is walking in here like she just made it through a goddess-be-damned bloodbath."

Wolf-boy? "What happened to Instructor Smexy Pants? 'Cause I could have sworn he was Instructor Smexy Pants yesterday."

Fiona speared me with a look that could peel paint. "Don't you sass me, Wren Acosta. I'm your de facto witchy BFF—not to be confused with your human BFF who is sitting on Hannah's couch right now—and I will not be deterred. I don't know if you've strolled past a mirror in the last five minutes, but you could pass for a fucking zombie."

"Ellie's here?" Sure, I'd given her a call when we'd finally gotten off that stupid mountain, but all I'd been able to do was leave a voicemail.

"Yes, and so is her mama, but before you go in there, I'm going to need some answers," Fiona said, fitting a fist on her hip. "And if you don't cough them up, Malia will have no problem gleaning them herself."

To her credit, Malia raised a single eyebrow and peeled off a glove.

My gaze drifted to Hannah who was resting her shoulder on the doorframe. She wasn't looking at me, either. No, she was staring at an equally bloody Nico like she'd really enjoy eating him for dinner.

But it wasn't me who answered. It was Nico. "My family made me choose between them and Wren. I chose Wren."

That hadn't exactly been what happened, but if that was how he saw it, I wouldn't be the one to change his mind. I was still trying to figure out what the fuck had just transpired myself, and why I felt light for maybe the first time in my life.

I mean, sure, there was a light show and everything, and the world kind of rocked, but I didn't know if what Diana said was true or not.

"What?" Hannah barked, standing straight. "They made you choose?"

"There was more to it than that," I said. *More like they slit my throat while he watched, but sure, we'll go with that.*

"Speaking of," Nico continued, "I need a place to stay. Would it be okay with everyone if I moved in with Wren downstairs?"

Normally, I'd hate that he hadn't asked me first, but this one time, I didn't give that first shit. I wanted

Nico with me—more than I could possibly put into words. Squeezing his fingers, I held on tight, praying no one had an issue.

If they did, well, then we'd just have to find somewhere else to stay. But we were sticking together.

"Of course," Fiona replied, wide-eyed. "We all sort of figured that if Wren was staying so were you."

It was a good assumption. I didn't think I wanted Nico out of my sight for a good long while, and I sure as hell wouldn't ever be going against his instincts ever again. Nico hadn't wanted me anywhere near Diana, and damn if his ass hadn't been right about that.

Then again, he thought meeting his family was a good idea, so maybe meeting people was just a bad idea for a while.

"Wren?" Ellie said before turning the corner, her eyes going wide as soon as she saw me. "Sweet mother of Mary, what happened to you?"

Ellie shouldered around Hannah and Fiona, gripping my arms harder than any human had a right to. "Please tell me this isn't your parents doing."

I had no idea why she jumped to that conclusion. My mother's tongue might be sharp, but it hadn't literally cut me before.

"As treacherous as they are, surprisingly no."

And considering that other than the PTSD from nearly getting my head lopped off, I was feeling positively awesome. Maybe that curse shit had merit. Maybe my parents were far more deceitful than I'd originally thought.

"Why do you think that?" Nico asked. It sounded a fuck of a lot like a demand, but after the day we'd had, I couldn't exactly blame him. He didn't need to put so much Alpha sauce on it, though.

Ellie's honey-brown eyes shifted from me to Nico and back again before falling to our entwined fingers. Eyebrows practically touching her forehead, she answered me instead of him. "Because they broke into our house looking for you. Or rather, your father came calling asking for you, and when we said we hadn't seen you, your mother blew up our door and walked in like she owned the place. They ripped our house apart searching for you."

Perfect. This was exactly what I wanted to deal with after damn near dying. Twice.

Sighing, I stared right at Malia without so much as a blink. "Please tell me you have alcohol."

A smile bloomed on Malia's face. "Vodka, tequila, whiskey, or gin?"

"Vodka," I replied, and Malia leapt off the stair

she was sitting on and raced to her apartment. Hopefully, she'd just give me the bottle because I was going to need it. I shifted my attention to Ellie. "Let me guess. This happened about forty-five minutes ago?"

Alice rounded the corner of Hannah's living room, her eyes the size of dinner plates before she shook herself. Alice was a nurse, she'd seen more shit than any human had a right to, and she'd already gotten the arcane crash course with me almost two decades ago.

"How did you know that?"

Nodding, I prayed Malia got me the vodka pronto. "Because forty-five minutes ago I was bleeding out on the floor and evidently breaking a twenty-year-old curse."

Malia tromped down the stairs, a vodka on the rocks in one hand and an iced, nearly full bottle in the other. She handed both over and I passed the glass to Nico. I flicked the top off the bottle and took a very long swig.

It meant that Diana was right. It meant that they *had* been cursing me, draining me, using me. And somehow, they didn't know where I was—at least for now.

Fabulous.

"Well, now I need to go tell a thousand-year-old

crazy woman that she was right and probably buy her a fucking fruit basket." I took another swig, swallowing down the welcomed burn. I wiped my mouth with the back of my hand. "But that's tomorrow's problem."

"That's never going to be your problem. You aren't telling that woman shit," Nico said into his glass right before he tilted his head back and drained it. Then he hooked a finger under my chin, leveling me with his gold stare. "Especially not 'thank you.' Not after what she did."

"Fair," I said on a sigh. One more round of introductions, and then I was taking a shower and drinking this bottle until it was empty. "Alice, Ellie, this is Nico. Nico, this is Ellie and Alice. Nico and I are... married."

Ellie chuckled. "Yeah, Fiona filled us in. Wren Acosta, huh? I like that a hell of a lot more than Bannister."

Funny, I did, too.

"It's a pleasure to meet you both," Nico said, nodding to each of them. "I've heard a lot of wonderful things about your family, and I'm grateful you were there for Wren growing up."

Alice waved at her tearing eyes. "Oh, stop. She was a dream child. She and Ellie both were. The gruesome twosome." She stepped closer, cupping both our cheeks like she was prone to do. "Couldn't have asked for better girls."

"If I wasn't covered in blood right now, I'd hug the shit out of both of you." Sucking in a deep breath, a pain in my heart eased. Meeting the parents hadn't gone so well for either of us, but having Nico meet Ellie and Alice? That was the best feeling in the world.

"Well, if there's anything my mama taught me it was how to get blood out of the wash," Fiona said, making me bust up laughing. Considering who Fiona's dad was, that did not surprise me one bit. "You need help, you let me know."

Somehow through the laughing, tears welled up in my eyes. "I love you guys. I really, really do. If the last few days have taught me anything, it's that blood relations can really let you down. Thanks for being here, for backing me up. For being my family."

Nico curled his arm around me, tucking me into his front as he pressed a kiss to my hair. "I'll always hug you, Bird. I don't care if you're bloody."

"My heart," Alice swooned, with both her hands pressed to her chest, like she was practically bursting with happiness. "He calls her 'Bird.' It's so freaking cute I can't stand it."

It wasn't a stretch to go from Wren to little bird. A wren was, in fact, a tiny bird, but I loved it when

Nico called me that. My belly did a dip, and my heart lurched every single time. I'd never had a nickname, and even though it was a small gesture of affection, it meant the world to me.

My eyes met Nico's and held. I was safe in this space. With family. I was safe in his arms. Nothing could hurt me here. And his scent filled my nose, reminding me that we were alive.

An emotion that felt like mine and *didn't* all at the same time, slammed into me. Yes, I felt that heaviness to my middle, that need, but now it seemed like there was gasoline poured on it. As if I wasn't just receiving my own emotions, but Nico's as well. Swallowing hard, I tried to focus on not jumping him in front of everyone. As much as I loved that Ellie was here and adored Alice, I had business to attend to.

"Well, that's our cue," Fiona said breezily. "They're doing the glowy-eyed stare thing."

"Glowy-eyed stare thing?" Alice asked. "Since when do Wren's eyes glow? Oh, dear, sweet baby Jesus, they *are* glowing."

Yeah, yeah, I was more of a weirdo now. I just couldn't muster the "give a fuck" for that one.

"Okay, we're going to bed. Love you guys." I yanked Nico by the hand toward the back staircase and glanced back at Ellie. "Call me tomorrow? We'll go get lunch, okay?" I got an excited, "Sure" before we rounded the corner and plodded down the stairs to my apartment.

As soon as the door closed, Nico shoved me against a wall, his arms bracketing my head as he leaned into my space. My blood was all over him—all over the both of us—but right then I didn't care. I didn't care that he'd somehow gotten my vodka bottle away from me. I didn't care that the scent of fear still clung to us or that we'd almost died.

Hell, maybe it was because we'd almost died. His lips devoured my own, his fingers tearing at my bloody shirt. My belly dipped as he ripped the fabric right down the middle, exposing my bra and stomach. A taloned finger trailed down my neck, in between my breasts, cutting through my bra with the efficiency of a razor.

Then his lips were on my skin, closing over my nipple, making me writhe. The rough stone walls scraped against my back, but I just couldn't make myself give a shit. A moment later, Nico had ripped my leggings off, somehow managing to get my shoes and socks, too. A part of me loved that he was dressed, and I was naked—loved that he needed to see all of me.

But I needed him, too. I needed him so much, I almost couldn't breathe. I grabbed the shoulder of his shirt and ripped, tearing the fabric as if it were tissue paper. I never wanted to see this shirt on him again. Because it wouldn't matter if we could get the stain out, I'd still know it was the shirt he'd been wearing when everything changed.

Nico stood, capturing my lips with his again, yanking me up his body by my thighs. And then we were moving. At that point, I didn't give a shit where we were going. I just wanted his lips on mine and his breath against my skin. I wanted him moving inside me, fucking every bad thought out of my head.

Because we were alive and safe and together, and that was all that mattered.

My fingers found his belt. That thing needed to go. And then I reached my prize, circling Nico's length, stroking him with my hand and wishing it was something else. I didn't really care if he was in my mouth or my pussy or my ass. I needed him inside me any way I could get him.

I needed it.

Then I wasn't holding him anymore. I was standing with my chest pressed against the wall and Nico's hand circling both my wrists above my head.

"So fucking impatient, aren't you?" he whispered in my ear, causing gooseflesh to rise all over my body. "You need me, beautiful? Is that it?"

I tried pressing back just to get a little contact, but he held me still.

"Answer me," he growled, sending a shot of lust through me so hard, my knees nearly buckled. Those were his emotions, his need. It seemed to double my own, making me almost mindless.

"Yes. I need you. Please, Nico. I need you."

His grip on my hands got tighter, making my sex clench. "What do you need? Tell me."

His hand cracked against my ass, sending a bolt of heat through me.

"I need you to fuck me. I need you inside me. I don't care where. I don't care how."

Nico's free hand found my hair, pulling my head back as he gripped my wrists tighter. "And what if I need to fuck you right here against this wall, huh? What if I need you bound and helpless while I fuck you every way I can think of?"

That sounded like the best idea.

"Yessssss," I hissed, trying to move, trying to get any contact whatsoever. But Nico held me still. So still, I fucking ached.

"Tie you up and fuck your mouth until you can't breathe. Take your ass. Make you beg."

I wanted every bit of that. "Yes. *Please*, Nico."

The hand in my hair moved to my throat, gripping my jaw in a hold that would be bruising, but

I just couldn't care. "You going to let me bite you, fuck you, make you mine?"

"*Yes*," I insisted, even though I was his already. I'd been his since he'd hauled me from the flames, I just hadn't known it yet.

He fit the tip of his cock against my opening, the combination of his words, his need, and my own, making me so fucking wet as he slid inside me to the hilt with very little resistance. I was so full, so full of him I could barely breathe, but it was so good I just didn't care.

Yes, we were still bloody. Yes, I was pressed against a rough stone wall. Yes, he was fucking me like a man possessed, fucking me so hard I almost couldn't breathe.

And I loved every minute of it.

My orgasm raced for me, cresting so fast I wasn't prepared, but Nico was. Right before it hit, he pulled out, making me whimper at the loss. A second later, we moved, and I found myself draped over a low-backed velvet armchair, the air kissing my ass and the slick wetness between my thighs.

I shifted, trying to find Nico, but his hand found my hair again, guiding my head down to his cock. Parting my lips, I took him in, tasting myself on his skin as I let him fuck my mouth. He wasn't gentle, and I didn't need him to be. I needed him rough, I needed him to make me, to make it hurt. To make me know he was mine and I was his and we were alive.

"Look at my beautiful little bird," he murmured, the praise in his voice making me wetter as his length filled my mouth. "Look at you, taking my cock so well. I love it when you moan around me."

As if on cue, I hummed out a moan. Maybe it was his command, or maybe it was his expert fucking fingers massaging oil in between my ass cheeks. Fuck it. I didn't care if I suffocated to death, I wanted him to keep doing whatever it was he was doing. And when had he gotten oil?

"You want me in your ass, don't you, Bird? You want me to fuck you everywhere, don't you?"

I moaned again, begging the only way I knew how.

Nico pulled himself from my mouth and circled me, his palm cracking against my ass when I tried moving against the chair. I needed relief. It was too much and too little, and every bit of his desire flooding our connection was making me crazy for him.

"Please fuck me. Please, Nico."

"Gods, you're so fucking sexy when you beg," he growled in my ear, the hint of his wolf coming out and making me shiver.

Then I felt him at the tight ring of muscle, the head of his cock pressing against me, breaching me, filling me so full. He eased in slowly, letting me adjust to him, taking care not to hurt me, even though I almost wanted the pain. Soon he was flush with my skin, and I was clawing at the chair, aching to move, needing something—anything.

I shoved back, making him move against me, making him thrust, and gods, it was so fucking good, I thought I was going to die. The moan that came out of me could have shattered the windows it was so loud. His hands found my wrists, pinning them behind my back as his thrusts got rougher, faster.

"Fuck, Wren. Fuck, you feel so fucking good."

His desire, his growls, his groans, his breath in my ear. I was so gone for him that every cell in my body was on fire. He could breathe on me, and I would be ready to go off. Nico's other hand skated down my body to my clit, and everything in me tightened. His thumb spread through my wetness before circling that bundle of nerves as his thrusts picked up the pace.

"You gonna come for me, little bird?"

It was as if my body was waiting for him to ask. Nico circled my clit one more time, and my orgasm slammed into me so hard I couldn't breathe, couldn't scream, couldn't move. Pleasure flooded my limbs, making me weak, but Nico held me up. He released my wrists and wrapped his arm across my chest, holding me to him like I was precious.

Then Nico struck, his bite searing into my skin, and his orgasm stole through us both so close after mine. It decimated me in a one-two punch. The noise that came out of my mouth sounded like I was being possessed.

Hell, maybe I was. Because Nico fucking owned me. He owned every cell in my body, every hair on my head. His heavy breaths in my ear, the way he held me so close, his praise all just made it that much more true.

I'd never in my life felt like this. Not for anyone. Like my heart was being ripped from my chest when they were gone, and it was put back to rights when they looked at me. Like their smile could change the course of an entire day. I'd never given myself over, never let someone be in charge, never wanted someone else to take what they needed.

And never in my life had I cared about someone —body and soul. Not like this.

A moment later, Nico slipped from me, coming back with a warm washcloth to clean me up.

My heart was so full, I thought I was going to cry.

Then I was in his arms, Nico cradling me like I

was precious, like I was special, like he had his whole world in his embrace.

"I think it's time for that shower, don't you?"

I loved him.

"Okay," I whispered, unsure of what to do next. I'd never loved anyone before—not like this.

I love him.

It seemed too big, too much. It scared me, how big it was.

Nico set me on the closed toilet lid and turned on the tap to the giant shower. We'd been just like this before in a cabin—him knowing what he was doing and me freaking out completely because I wholeheartedly did not.

He knelt at my feet, closing the distance between us, hooking his fingers under my chin so I had to look at him.

"I love you, Wren."

No one—no boyfriend—had ever told me that before. I'd never made it to the full relationship, "fall in love" stage. It took a minute for my brain to compute.

"Good. That's good." The relief I felt, the joy. It felt like my heart was going to beat out of my chest.

"Because you love me, too?" He said it with such confidence, it made me wonder if he could read my mind.

Nodding, I whispered, "Yes. So much."

Nico's expression softened, and it was as if the sun was shining on me. "Then tell me, Bird. Tell me you love me."

So, I did.

CHAPTER THIRTEEN

NICO

The last time I woke up to Wren not in my bed, I panicked. I raced to find her and acted like a grade-A jackass in the process. This time was no different. My heart beat out of my chest at the feel of the cool sheets against my skin, sending alarm bells through me.

Where is she?

Did I dream it?

Is she even alive?

The memory of the blood pouring from her neck, of her gasping breaths, burned through my brain. Of not being able to get to her, of hearing her heart slow, watching her eyelids flutter closed. Begging her to stay with me.

It was as if I was still in my father's study holding on to Wren for dear life, praying if she went, someone would do me the favor of killing me, too.

My gut twisted, sweat beaded on my forehead, and I knifed out of bed, ready to tear the world apart to find her. My wolf howled at me, but I couldn't focus on him or what he was saying. I couldn't do anything but scan the room and know she wasn't there.

That was until I heard the sizzle and pop of bacon cooking on the stove, the scent finally hitting my nose through the panic.

She's alive. It wasn't a dream. She's alive.

But I needed to see it for myself. Snatching my jeans from the bedside chair, I shoved my legs into them and stalked to find Wren, not bothering to button or really zip them up.

Around the stone wall was a fully equipped galley kitchen with all the bells and whistles. And right at the stove in one of my T-shirts was Wren. Her red hair was piled on her head, a thick tendril escaping the bun and trailing down her neck.

Gods, she was fucking beautiful.

Headphones in her ears, she bounced to loud rock music as she transferred the bacon to a paper-towel-covered plate, my shirt riding up to give the best view of her naked ass. I could have watched her forever, but my dick had many, many other plans.

I stalked closer, wrapped an arm around her waist, and turned off the burner. She didn't seem surprised at my approach, rather that she'd known I'd been there the whole time. Wren popped her earbuds out, paused her music, and looked up at me. The now-paused song had been blasting at eardrum-shattering levels. How had she known I was there?

"About time you woke up. I was about to start the eggs. How many do you want and how do you like them?"

So innocent, so pure. I could have bathed in it if it were possible to have this much goodness. I just prayed I didn't ruin it.

Turning her in my arms, I hooked my hands under her thighs and yanked her up my body. Instantly, she wrapped her legs around my hips, and I got delicious handfuls of her luscious ass.

"We'll get to the eggs later," I growled, prowling out of the kitchen and back to bed. I put a knee in the mattress, returning Wren exactly where she should have stayed. Settling in between her thighs, I bunched the fabric of her shirt in my hands, tearing it off in one big rip.

There.

That was better.

Wren's eyes rounded even as her scent grew sweeter. "Nico, I—"

"How about when I'm sleeping, you don't leave this bed without waking me up?" It was an order, yes, but I hoped it had come out softer than it sounded in my head. "I know I'm being unreasonable. I know, Bird. I just... I need this. I don't care if it's to go to the bathroom or to make breakfast. I swear to you that I don't need the sleep. Waking up without you next to me..."

I shook my head, unable to properly articulate just how bad it was. "Every time I close my eyes, I see you bleeding. I wake up without you there, and it's as if saving you was the dream and I'm waking up to realize that you're really gone."

Wren's expression softened as she softly cupped my cheeks. "If that's what you need, then that's what you need." She drew me down, pressing her lips against my own, the heat of her skin against mine making my eyes roll up into my head. "I won't leave without waking you." She nipped at my bottom lip. "Promise."

Her feet unwrapped from around my back, and she started trying to shove my jeans down my legs— not too hard a task since I hadn't bothered to button the damn things. Still, I helped, guiding my cock to her opening and sliding in with a single long stroke.

Wren gasped into my mouth, her glowing green-gold eyes shining as her perfect legs wrapped me up like a fucking present. Our bodies pressed together, her eyes on mine, her gasps in my ears, it reminded me that she was really here.

She's alive. It wasn't a dream. She's alive.

My hands in her hair, her lips on mine, we moved together slowly, leisurely savoring every touch, every kiss, every moan.

She's alive.

Her eyes fluttered closed as she tilted her head back in the bed, but even that—

"Look at me," I demanded, sitting back on my knees and taking her with me. I needed to know it was real. That she was safe. I focused on the way her eyes flashed open, warming with a new heat as I took her harder, faster. "Watch what you do to me."

But she didn't obey me this time. Instead, she cupped my face and kissed my lips. "I'm really here, Nico. I'm with you. I'm alive."

Wrapping her in my arms, I hugged her to me, breathing her in, letting that jasmine and honey scent fill my nose as proof. Her heart pounded against mine as I thrust harder, swallowing her moans as we moved together.

When she was close, her eyes lit up, brighter than I'd ever seen, and when she smiled, a double set of upper and lower fangs lengthened her canines.

Holy shit.

She wasn't a wolf, and yet somehow, she drew on mine just enough to—

In a flash, Wren struck, her fangs breaking my skin like I had done so many times to her. Heat raced up my spine, tightening my balls, sending gooseflesh breaking out all over my skin. My release raced for me, barreling toward me like a freight train.

She released my shoulder, her mouth bloody and so fucking sexy I thought I was going to explode. Naturally, I did the only thing that I knew would send her over the edge. My own fangs sliced into her flesh, cementing her mark—our marks—in a way that could never be broken.

Wren's moan was guttural as she came, her nails clawing into my skin. I couldn't hold myself back anymore. Releasing her shoulder, I brought her face to mine, kissing her with everything I had, mingling our blood together as our tongues twined.

She's alive.

And I'd have proof that Wren was mine for the rest of my life.

· · ·

Over the next couple of days, Wren and I ordered takeout, purchased an inordinate number of things for our new apartment, filled out her wardrobe, and hung out with Fiona, Hannah, Malia, and Ellie. I refused to think about my family, Wren refused to hear a word about hers, and we adjusted to living together. Most disagreements were solved via orgasms, and I folded far more than I thought possible to a woman half a foot shorter than me.

The six of us were piled in my and Wren's apartment while Wren and Ellie finished up dinner —the pair shooing me out of the kitchen after I kept eating the tomatoes from Wren's sauce. Hannah and I were discussing the merits of certain hunting techniques at the dining table we'd moved into the courtyard, while Fiona and Malia were playing a witchy sort of game reminiscent of bocce ball that involved alcohol and floating orbs.

"Okay, people. Soup's on," Wren said as she laid a platter the size of a trough filled with pasta and fish and a creamy tomato sauce on the table. Her green sundress clung to her curves while the thin straps tried to fall down her shoulders.

As soon as the food was safe, I yanked her onto my lap, half-irritated that she hadn't asked me to help her carry it and half-amazed at this woman's cooking. Because Wren could *cook*. She'd made every single

Portuguese recipe she could get her hands on because she wanted me to feel like home, and when she found out that my mom always switched up the traditional ones to include Southern flavor, Wren went off.

I couldn't get her ass out of the kitchen. At this rate, I was going to eat my weight in glorious food every night, and I just could not bring myself to think that was a bad thing.

"Thank you for the food, Bird. But if you try to do the dishes, I'm spanking your ass."

Wren turned, planted a quick kiss to my lips and slid into her own seat. "Don't you threaten me with a good time. But if you want to do the dishes, I won't stop you. That kitchen is a mess."

Wren was a good cook but a messy cook. She had some sort of chef magic that made every ounce of food she prepared end up a goddamn miracle, but she'd use every dish in the house to do it.

Ellie sighed, propping her head on her fist. "Wren said you've got brothers. You got any single ones that aren't murderous douche bags and don't mind human graduate students with time-management issues?"

I'd learned that now that Alice wasn't deathly ill, Ellie was now planning on going back to school for her master's in social work. But she had an essay to turn in on what she'd been doing for the last two years. She'd been hemming and hawing over it for three days.

"You'll meet the deadline, El. You can do this," Fiona said with a wink as she took her seat. "And if you don't, I know a guy who can help you out if you know what I'm saying."

I chose to ignore both statements—both the brother talk and the "knowing a guy" business. We only had a few more days before we'd have to report to the ABI—I was on leave, thankfully—and I had managed to not think about my family while Wren and I stayed wrapped in our little bubble.

I'd ignored calls from Wyatt and my brothers, only taking the ones from my mom, but even those ended after she tried to convince me to come home. I understood where she was coming from. No mother wanted strife between her children, and no Alpha's wife wanted a feud in her own home. But the Acosta house wasn't home anymore, and after what they had done, it never would be again.

"I didn't hear that," I grumbled, taking a swig of my beer.

Fiona stuck out her tongue. "I meant on the college admissions board, you weirdo."

Wren pointed the tongs at her. "You've lived in

Savannah less than a week and you already know someone on the college admissions board?"

Fiona shrugged, sniffing as she held out her plate. "I'm personable. People like me."

That part was true. Fiona was a good egg, even being from a notorious family.

Malia snorted into her drink. "More like she makes it her business to know important people all around town so when she needs to question them later, she has all the dirt."

Fiona smacked her shoulder. "You stinker. You weren't supposed to tell anyone."

"Oh, please," Hannah said, dishing up her own plate. Funnily enough, ghouls only ate the *other, other* white meat about every six months or so. "You are not as subtle as you think you are. It's just those boys see your blonde hair and tiny waist and they're complete goners. You don't even need to prime them. It's just sad."

Fiona was nothing if not proactive. And the way she'd warded this house? It was a work of art. No one who didn't already know our address would be able to find it. Their eyes would pass right over it as if it wasn't there.

We laughed through dinner, filling our bellies with fabulous food and wine, and at the end of the night, Wren sat on the counter while I did the dishes.

We made love and got to know each other and breathed. It was the happiest time in my life.

So, when Serreno showed up at our door at four thirty in the morning, it was more than a surprise. And when she told us what was at stake, it was a wonder we didn't hear from her before now.

I should have known. And if I had, there would have been no way Wren and I would have stayed a single day in Savannah.

But it was already too late.

CHAPTER FOURTEEN

WREN

The doorbell woke me up before dawn two days before Nico and I were supposed to report in at the ABI field office. I'd been oscillating between dreading it and being so excited I couldn't sit still in equal measure. It would be my very first arcane job, and considering I wasn't being drained or cursed anymore—not that I quite knew what that meant yet—I was hopeful.

We had a stash of Ames' null amulets on standby, but I wondered if I'd even need them now. Fiona hadn't had much trouble casting around me since the throat-slitting debacle, but I wasn't sure if that was just because she adjusted her spells to account for the added magic in the air or if I wasn't a magical time bomb anymore.

Personally, I was scared to find out.

And since Fiona had locked down our property so tight it was a wonder air got in, the ringing of the doorbell was a bit of a shock. Given that no one could find our house without already knowing where it was, whoever was on the other side of that door had to be very powerful, very smart, very patient, or a friend.

But anyone coming to call at four thirty in the damn morning had to be bringing bad tidings.

Nico and I dressed in a hurry, tossing on whatever we'd peeled off each other the night before. Nico pulled on his jeans and a T-shirt while I struggled with my dress for about three seconds before giving up and going for yoga pants and a tank with a built-in bra.

Barefoot and freaked, I followed Nico up the stairs—much to his chagrin.

"I told you—"

"Look here, Wolf Man. You can be assured that I'm safe with you, or you can freak the fuck out because you can't see me and be off your game. You remember the Italian restaurant?"

Nico had damn near lost it because I was in the bathroom too long at this little place down on the

River Walk. The place was packed, and the line took an age. By the time I got out, Nico was outside the bathroom waiting on me and damn near sweating through his shirt, he'd been panicking so bad.

I didn't want to bring it up, but not being at his side freaked me the fuck out, too. Call it codependent if you wanted to, but our shit was trauma bonded to the nth degree and that wouldn't be breaking anytime soon.

His glowing eyes flashed in the dim stairwell. "Fine."

Yeah, I was going to pay for that later, probably with some spankings or getting tied up or—

"Would you quit it? Gods, woman, I cannot deal with you thinking about how I'm going to punish you later. I can't concentrate with my dick hard as granite."

Sticking out my tongue, I followed him up the stairs, the mirth leaving me as soon as our boss came into view. Erica Serreno was resplendent in a rust-colored suit and cream silk blouse, her dark twists piled on her head in a complicated style. She held a steaming coffee cup in one hand and a paper shopping bag in the other.

There was something rotten in the bag, too, and I had a feeling I didn't want to know what it was.

"Wren, Nico, sorry to interrupt the last of your vacation, but—"

"You have a severed body part in that bag," Hannah finished for her, emerging from the kitchen holding her own steaming mug.

How either of them could be drinking coffee at a time like this was fucking astounding. And who needed coffee? The sheer fact that my boss was in my house, holding a severed body part was enough to wake me all the way the fuck up.

"I'm sorry. You what?" I asked, whipping my head back in Serreno's direction, really, really hoping I heard Hannah wrong.

Before Serreno could answer me, two sets of footsteps clomped down the stairs. Fiona came first, her blonde hair in a messy bun on top of her head, silk eye mask pulled up on her forehead, a fuzzy purple robe sinched tight on her waist with matching slippers on said feet, so her clomps were more of a shushing sound, but whatever.

Malia, however, had let her hair free of its usual sleek bun, the curls fanning up and out in a lion's mane of black coils. Normally so buttoned up, it was especially weird to see her in a holey sweatshirt with a collar stretched so wide it fell off one shoulder and a pair of oversized men's pajama bottoms. Barefoot, her stomps were hard enough they hurt my own feet by proxy. She yawned wide as she rubbed her eyes with her gloved hand, not bothering to open them as she trundled down to Hannah's level.

"There better be a good gods-damned reason you're waking me up at four thirty in the fucking morning. Someone better be dead."

Eyebrows raised, I shared a grave look with Nico, and he tightened his hold on my hand. He hadn't said a word since coming up the stairs, and I had a feeling he was thinking the same damn thing.

"Funny you should say that," Serreno replied, her smooth voice the picture of calm. "I need you to find out."

Malia's lids popped open, spearing Serreno with a glare fit to peel paint. "Excuse me? I'm not even on the job yet, and you want me to do what, exactly?"

Serreno's shoulders took on a steely set, solidifying into pure determination as she firmed her jaw. "As Agent Dumond so dutifully pointed out, I have human remains in this bag. I need you to tell me if the person belonging to them is alive, and if possible, where they are."

Malia stopped six stairs from the bottom, getting no closer to the bag or Serreno. "The fuck you do. I did not sign up to touch dead things, ma'am. It is written specifically in my contract. Give me one good reason I shouldn't go back to bed right now."

Serreno narrowed her eyes and took a sip of coffee, seeming to gather her strength.

"I second this," Nico said, his tone pure malice. "You don't announce yourself—you don't talk to the senior agent on the premises, you just show up at the ass crack of dawn with a severed body part in tow and expect us to jump to? In my den? With people under my protection? What the fuck, Erica?"

Serreno drained her cup before setting it on the entryway table. "Look, I would love to follow social norms and all, but I have an agent missing her foot, and said foot was hand delivered by a spelled human, high on that new Fae drug we've been trying to keep out of the college dorms since last August. The damn kid handed over a box and a note and then proceeded to OD in the middle of the lobby and skip on over to the afterlife before we could get him the antidote."

"Shiiiit," I said, parking my ass on the bench right beside the stair landing.

"Oh, it gets worse," Serreno bit out. "That note? It offers the agent belonging to this foot in exchange for Wren. Signed and everything. The name Desmond ring any bells with you?"

I was glad I was already sitting down because the world started spinning. I'd done my best to try and forget—just for a little while—that Desmond even existed. Girard's warnings about his dark Fae buyer seemed so fantastical, they felt more like whimsical bullshit to save his own ass than anything else. But faced with the reality of him made me physically ill.

"Now, all told, I have thirty agents and fourteen students missing based off my calculations, and those calculations are a fucking wag because Girard's penchant for keeping off the radar surpasses known heights. It calls into question every single person that did not make it out of Blue Ridge for the last thirty years. Every single agent who left to go on assignment, every single one who decided to leave the Bureau for good. Every single one who got transferred."

I wasn't looking at the director, but I felt her stare. Forty-four people. That they knew of. Just gone. Forty-four women taken. Sweat broke out all over my skin as the lights in the room flickered. My tongue felt heavy in my mouth as saliva pooled, the scent of rotten meat filling my nose.

Nico's hand felt like knives on my skin as he rubbed my back, his words garbled in my ears as panic set in.

Forty-four women. And I had almost been one of them. And she was right. Girard had covered his tracks. When Fiona had gone missing, it was almost as if she'd never been to Blue Ridge at all. Even her scent had been wiped away. According to Nico, her records were clean, and if he hadn't already known something was up and I hadn't kept pushing...

A bucket appeared right in front of my face, and I latched onto it before losing what little I had in my stomach. I'd sort of shoved everything that had happened with Girard down somewhere deep, and now it was coming up vomit-style.

Forty-four women.

I heaved until there was nothing left, but still, my stomach wanted to revolt. Forty-four women. And Fiona and I had almost been among them. Forty-four women never searched for. Forty-four women never missed. People with no families or on the outs with them, I'd bet. People who wouldn't have someone looking for them.

Forty-four women stolen. Sold. Used. Like property. Like chattel. All to line Girard's pockets. If I had anything left in my stomach, I would have thrown up more.

A cold washcloth appeared as if by magic in front of my face, and I wiped my skin as if it would wash away how fucking dirty I felt. Nico took it from me and handed me a cup of mouthwash. Blissfully, I took that, too, rinsing my mouth and spitting into the bucket.

My gaze found Fiona's, and just like me, she

looked ill. Like me, she was probably wondering if things had gone different if she'd be reduced to a severed foot in a bag. A lonely clue in a case so big it was a wonder how it had ever been a secret. Fiona's knuckles were white as she gripped the railing, her skin so pale it was a wonder she was standing.

"So, I need to know if this particular agent is still alive, and if this foot actually fucking belongs to her." Serreno's shoulders fell. "You know, six months ago, I told another agent that something like this could never happen here. That we could never have corruption go on under our noses to the degree of the Knoxville branch. Kenzari told me I'd eat my words one day, that I'd need her help and she wouldn't be able to give it to me. And damn if that fucking oracle wasn't right."

I didn't know who this Kenzari person was, but damn if she hadn't been right on this one. Because even I'd heard of the Knoxville dust-up—everyone had. Werewolf wars, death mages on a power trip, European vampires trying to take over. It had me wondering how they were keeping all of this under wraps.

"Look, I'm sorry you seem to have an internal problem, but I specifically said no dead things." Malia descended the last six steps, crossing her arms over her chest. "As I recall, you agreed. Personally. So you're telling me you're reneging on our deal?"

Serreno's eyes flashed, not with magic but with challenge. "Technically speaking, I don't know if the person that belongs to this is dead or not. One could make a case against a breach of contract."

Malia narrowed her eyes, her jaw firming to granite. "One year's worth of wages as a bonus for every body part read."

"Six months," Serreno haggled, eyeing the small psychometry witch like she was a particularly sharp thorn in her shoe.

Malia's unhinged laugh was a thing of nightmares. "A year. Mostly to pay for the fucking therapy I'll need after this."

Serreno growled as she gnashed her teeth. "Fine. A year. But this better be good. I want everything you can give me."

Malia's lip curled as she skirted around the director and headed for Hannah's kitchen, disappearing around the corner. "You'll get what you get, and I expect that money to be in my bank account by noon, or I'm ripping up our contract and going to work for Fiona's dad," she threatened, likely pouring herself a cup of coffee from Hannah's probably nearly empty pot. "Which side of the line do you want me on, boss?"

CHAPTER FIFTEEN

WREN

I had a feeling that working for Fiona's dad wouldn't exactly put Malia in the driver's seat of her own life, but that was just me.

"I'll call accounting as soon as you give me what I need," Serreno bit out. "Will that make you happy, Agent Nadir?"

Malia emerged from Hannah's kitchen, sipping on a mug of steaming brew. "Not a gods-damned thing about this morning has made me happy, but sure. I'm peachy fucking keen."

Serreno reached into the bag, removing a pale-gray foot encased in a plastic Zip-lock.

"Whoa, no," Nico barked. "Don't you dare open

that thing in here. It's bad enough you're bringing this here. You open that inside and we'll never get the smell out. Courtyard, Erica. Now."

Nico dropped a kiss to my forehead as he rested his palms on my shoulders. "Give us a minute, would you?" Shakily, I nodded, hanging back, and he shifted his eyes to Hannah. "Don't let her out of your sight, you got me?"

Hannah gave him the middle finger salute, but stayed right by my side as he moved to Erica, roughly grabbing his boss' arm and dragging her downstairs.

"I swear I'm going to need to bleach my nose after this," Malia grumbled before draining her mug.

But I couldn't look at her or Hannah who was absolutely watching me like a hawk. I'd slipped my leash once and I'd probably never live that shit down. No, my gaze found Fiona's again. It was one thing to be kidnapped by Girard. It was a whole other to have body parts of agents just floating around.

Fi descended the rest of the way down the stairs, reaching for my hand. I took it, praying that we found the poor woman, but also... I sort of hoped when we found her, she was at rest. It was a terrible thing to almost wish for someone's death, but sometimes, it was better to be dead.

Because despite what the world wanted you to believe, sometimes death wasn't the worst thing.

"That poor agent," Fiona whispered, shaking her head. "You don't think she's still breathing, do you? Stuck wherever that guy Desmond is?"

I had a sinking feeling in my belly that was exactly where she'd been for however long she'd been gone.

"Okay, let's get this shit over with. Hannah?" Malia asked as she directed her feet to my staircase. "Bring the vodka and the bleach, will you? I'll watch these two bozos until then, yeah?"

Hannah brought two fingers to her eyes and then pointed them at me.

Yeah, yeah. I was the problem child in this scenario. "I got it."

Following Malia down the stairs, I nearly gagged at the scent of rotten flesh coming from the courtyard. I had half a mind to run away screaming if I was being honest.

"You aren't trading her," Nico hissed, his voice as clear to me as if he were right next to my ear. "It's bad enough you still don't know why there was a termination entered onto her sentence when we both know Wren's crime didn't deserve that. Now this? I don't know what you think you're doing—"

"Of course not," Serreno said, cutting him off. "Agent Lewis might have been a powerful illusion mage, but there is no way I'm trading one woman for another. Not only is that completely unethical, but there is no way to know what the ramifications are with Wren's abilities. It would be like giving a dark Fae a fucking nuke. No, thank you. And I'm pretty sure the order was Girard's backup plan. If he couldn't get her one way, he was going to fail her, pretend to execute her, and hand her over. But that's just a guess since I can't find any records where that was her actual sentence."

Nico shot me a look over Serreno's shoulder, his gold eyes flashing in the dark. "And Wren's family?"

"Still causing problems, but since their wardings and spells are literally crumbling, half of Savannah has been scrambling to fill the void. Wren should be glad she got out of that family when she had the chance. I have a feeling the witch community is going to cannibalize them soon enough."

For once, I didn't feel even a little guilty at leaving the lot of my family behind. Not a single one of them ever came to my aid, never gave a kind word, never tried to help me. Would I feel different if they had? If it were Ellie or Alice instead?

Probably.

But if they happened to get their comeuppance after years of abuse? Well, I wouldn't be stepping in to save them.

"Come on," Malia urged, skirting around Fi and I

as we dawdled in my bedroom. "Let's get this shit over with."

I moved to follow, but Fiona tightened her grip on my hand. "You don't have to stay here—neither of us do. I'll call my dad. He can get us out of Savannah in an hour if we need to. Go to Tennessee where the Fae are sparse. Just until the heat's off."

But all the while, I kept my gaze locked on Nico's. "If you think you need to go, I want you to be safe. But the only way I'm leaving is if it's with Nico."

The glow of Nico's irises built as if his wolf was looking out of Nico's eyes, staring right at me.

I'm not leaving. I'm not going anywhere. I won't go looking for trouble. Not by myself. Not ever again.

Knowing what I knew now, I wouldn't leave him without a damn good explanation and I sure as shit wouldn't go off half-cocked.

Nico deserved better than that.

Fiona sighed, loosening her grip on my fingers. "That's what I figured you'd say. And if he tells you to leave?"

"Then he needs to toss me over his shoulder and move me himself." I was completely serious, but the wide smile that pulled at Nico's lips made my heart race and my belly do a somersault.

"Okay," Malia said, settling onto one of the patio chairs. "Give me the damn thing."

If I thought the stench was bad inside the bag, it was nothing compared to when Serreno opened it. Both Fiona and I gagged, and we were barely within fifty feet. Hannah came up from behind us, and even she looked a little ill.

"Jesus, fuck. That is rancid," she groaned.

Another fun fact I learned about ghouls? They preferred fresh meat, not long-dead meat. Sure, they'd eat it if they had to, but it was a lot like me eating liver and onions. Like, sure, it was food, but no one thought it was a high-quality meal.

Personally, I'd take the liver over this.

Serreno and Nico must have ironclad stomachs because they appeared completely unfazed. Like this was just another Tuesday. Braving a glance, I forced myself to not avert my gaze. Whoever this woman was, she deserved me to at least witness what I could.

The flesh was grayer outside of the bag than in, the severed edge rough like it had been torn off rather than cut. And if I had a guess, this was what gangrene looked like before it was excised for life-saving purposes.

Malia held out a single finger, bare now that she'd stripped off her glove, and touched it to the exposed mottled flesh. As soon as she made contact, it was as if she'd been hit by a bolt of lightning. She jolted, her entire body going rigid as her eyes rolled into the back of her head.

"A-agent Penelope Lewis, i-illusion ma-mage, taken from Blue Ridge twenty-five years ago." She sucked in a breath, her brow furrowing like she was in pain. "R-rah-reported as deep undercover with only t-top-level access to her file. But she n-never made it."

Malia's body seized, her nose bloody and dripping down her front. I shoved past Fiona and Hannah and yanked Nico's shirt from his back, ripping the fabric to cover my hands. Only then did I touch her. Malia had to know she didn't have to do this alone. As soon as my hands landed on her shoulders, her breath eased, her shoulders relaxed. But she was hurt. I could smell the blood, so I pushed, giving over a little bit of power like I'd done with Nico.

Malia sighed as if I helped, and I hoped I did, but I couldn't be too sure.

"G-girard nearly caved in her skull before delivering her to a man. She never saw his face. He told her to make him see, but Penelope was too scared, too new. As powerful as she was, she was too green, too new and hadn't figured out how to tune her magic to Fae eyes. He was so mad that she couldn't make pretty pictures for him, so he told her to dance. S-she did. She d-danced until her feet were bloody and her body gave out. He'd wait for her to be rested, and she'd do it all over again."

A Fae could see through most magics, and illusions were the easiest for them to spot. It made no sense that a Fae would want an illusionist to keep. Not unless he enjoyed torturing young women.

Malia grabbed my covered hand with her own, squeezing it tight as she came out of her trance. Her whole body shook, faint tremors of whatever it was she'd seen. She started to sit up, but I gently pushed her back down. She was still bleeding from her nose and ears, and her body was sipping at my power, trying to revive itself.

"I don't know if she's alive, but if you were wondering if that foot belongs to a Penelope Lewis, you have the right agent. And if you want to look for her, I suggest you start in the Fae realm."

Nico grabbed my shoulder, spinning me around, so that I was staring right at his glowing golden eyes. "Don't even think about it, Bird. You hear me. This is one area where you can't help."

Is he high? Malia just described my worst nightmare, and he thinks I'm going to what, just hand myself over?

"I made a deal with Carmichael Jones instead of going to the River Walk to talk to the Fae on purpose. I'm sorry about the agent, I really am, but hell no." I shifted my attention to Serreno. "I don't know what you think of me, but I am not, in fact, a martyr. That shit with Girard was a fluke. No offense, Fi, but I did not get kidnapped on purpose. The only reason I went into his cabin at all was because I thought I knew where he was. I'll sacrifice for my friends, sure. Nico? Absolutely. But this agent? I'm so sorry, but there is no way on this earth or any other I'm giving myself up to save a stranger. Especially to a dark Fae. This is one area where you do not have to worry about me."

Serreno bit her lip as she tried to hold in a snicker.

"Plus, did you see that foot? That was not severed with a sharp knife. That shit was torn the fuck off. That woman is more than likely dead as a doornail. I am not skipping off to get kidnapped anytime soon to save a dead girl. No. *No.*" My eyes speared Serreno. "And if you think you're about to offer me a bonus, you can keep it. There isn't a payment big enough to make me hand myself over to my worst nightmare. No, thank you."

Nico wrapped me up in his arms, his laugh wildly inappropriate but welcome all the same. "I fucking love you, Bird. You know that?"

At that moment, I really, really did.

But I met Malia's gaze over his shoulder, and as

much as I loved the way he was holding me right now, her haunted expression told me she hadn't quite shared everything with us. Twenty-five years of pain. Twenty-five years of torture and fear. I squeezed Nico and gently pushed him away. Malia and Fiona and Hannah needed me right now.

I knelt by her chair. "How about a scalding-hot bath followed by some mind bleach? I know I have some tequila around here somewhere, yeah? When you're ready, I'll even make you some soup or something. Some bread from scratch? I have a loaf rising in the fridge already."

Malia's expression was grateful, but the horrors she'd seen were still playing behind her eyes.

Yeah, she'd need all the therapy in the world and then some.

And maybe even that wasn't enough.

CHAPTER SIXTEEN

NICO

I'd never been so pissed at my boss in my fucking life. It made no sense for her to come here, none whatsoever. Did I hate that Lewis was missing? Yes, but she'd been gone for twenty-five fucking years and *now* they were pressed about looking for her?

If it hadn't been for Wyatt sticking his nose into this shit, no one would have even known what was going on. His curiosity had started a domino effect, changing both Wren's and my life mostly for the better. But that didn't mean we owed the Bureau our souls for it, and it sure as shit didn't mean that we needed to sacrifice for their oversight.

Wren's copper hair was piled on her head as she paced our apartment. She had that look about her like she was about to ask me something, and if I couldn't feel her gut burning with anxiety, I would have made her quit already. We'd spent the better part of yesterday apart, my presence not necessarily all too welcome in a sea of estrogen and chocolate and tacos.

Malia was a far sight closer to crazy than she had been the night before, and whatever she saw from Lewis' flesh, I was very happy to not know. But Wren needed to help her friend, and I had to be a good mate.

Even though I hated to be apart from her.

Even though I wanted her to myself.

Even though I feared what she might do next.

Sure, Wren had said she wouldn't give herself up, but she'd also told me she wasn't going to give Dumond a hard time or leave the safety of numbers or go investigate Girard. I didn't know how much I trusted that my little bird's hero streak wouldn't rear its ugly head.

"Okay, Bird," I said, picking her up mid-pace and depositing her onto the bed before covering her with my body. "What has you in a twist? Is it Malia? The missing agents or—"

"I'm scared to go to work," she blurted, her lips

screwing up into a grimace. "I know the curse is gone, but what does that mean? Can people do magic around me or not? Fiona seems to have figured it out, but... What happens if I go into the ABI building and shit starts blowing up? I mean, Ames' null wards work, sure, but not for very long, and—"

I dropped a kiss to her still-moving lips, nipping at the bottom one just to ease a little of her fear. "So you aren't thinking about the other shit? Just first-day jitters?"

"Well," Wren said, blinking like my question was a little odd, "yeah. I mean I'm worried about Malia, but other than being her friend, I can't do much about that. And the missing agent shit is being handled by people well above my pay grade. Do I want to help? Of course I do. But other than getting coffee, doing scut work, and burying myself in paperwork, there isn't much else I have to offer. I wouldn't even know where to start."

I had a feeling she totally would know where to start and probably direct a few agents to look in the right direction, but that was just me.

"I'm more worried about what happens when they find out I wouldn't... wouldn't... hand myself over for her. And what if they find out I'm an amplifier? And... are they going to look at me funny for marrying my instructor? Even though I totally maintain that I require a pretty dress and a ring and all the bells and whistles to be fully considered married, but whatever."

Oh, she was getting the dress and the ring and a big dinner with all the people we cared about. I just hadn't had the time to give any of it to her. Though, I had picked up the ring yesterday while she was making tacos. It was a brilliant oval-cut sapphire—the color of the same moonlit night when I'd made her mine.

Though the glowing crescent mark on her shoulder was proof enough, she'd get her ring. She'd get anything she wanted, anything I could give her, anything in my power.

"So let me see if I have this straight. You're worried about work, how people will think of you, and whether or not you'll hurt someone while you're there?"

Wren gave me a little shrug, her perfect white teeth nibbling on her bottom lip.

"Well, I can help with a few of those things. Why don't we get dressed and go down to Factors Walk? You can see how magic reacts around you in the open. We'll bring some of Ames' null wards just in case, and then you'll know how everything will work."

Wren seemed a little skeptical, but hopeful, too.

Maybe it would work, and if it didn't, well, we'd figure something out.

"I can't predict how other people see you, but wolf matings are pretty commonplace. No one will think twice about me being your instructor, and once they know you're mated to an Acosta, no one in their right mind would assume you'd give yourself up. Or that I would just sit idly by while my wife skipped off to the Fae realm."

"I just keep thinking that everyone is going to be staring at me the second I walk in there. I'm a Bannister for fuck's sake."

I fit a hand under her neck, squeezing just a little so she'd pay attention.

"No, you aren't. They never inducted you into their coven, they never treated you like family. You share their blood and that's it, Bird. You're an Acosta. It's on your badge and everything. And Acostas don't give a fuck what other people think. You're just as much an Alpha as I am. A fierce protector, a strong, capable leader. Plus," I said, turning us both so she was on top, "if anyone says shit to you, I'll be right there to rip their hearts from their chest."

And I was only half-kidding about that one. Okay, I wasn't kidding. I was so on edge if someone looked at her funny, death was a definite possibility.

"So, let's get dressed and take a walk. Then we can worry about something else. Deal?"

Wren dropped a smoldering kiss to my lips, and it was a struggle to remember that we were supposed to be doing something. Oh, that was right. Leaving the apartment. Somehow, we made it outside, laughing at silly, stupid shit as we tromped down to Factors Walk. It was a hike, but parking down there was a nightmare.

We held hands and stopped at food vendors and shared our finds. It was only when we'd traversed the treacherous stairs down to The Walk that Wren's good mood seemed to dissipate.

"You know, the last time I walked down these steps, I almost face-planted," she said, holding onto my hand so tight it was a wonder blood was making it to the tips of my fingers. "I was so nervous thinking Alice was going to die that I almost broke my neck on these stupid cobblestones."

"I remember," I murmured, pulling her under my arm. "I was trailing a spike in dark magic, and it led me straight to you. I remember seeing you, so nervous, so determined. You were going to that apothecary, and you were getting what you needed."

"Then the fire," she whispered, resting her head on my shoulder.

Her gaze drifted in the direction of where Azalea

Apothecary used to stand. In its place was a brand-new apothecary owned by the Horne twins after they bought the land right out from under Carmichael Jones. In a little over two weeks, they'd completely rebuilt the place, and the witch and warlock community was in an uproar about it. Considering the Horne twins had bought out every other apothecary in town except for Jones' place, it was a big fucking deal.

The ABI was just waiting for shit to pop off before stepping in. If there was one thing the arcane community hated, it was a monopoly.

"I don't know why I thought it was still going to be a shell, but..." She shook her head. "I almost wanted proof it happened. Everything was such a whirlwind, I barely had time to grasp it, you know?"

And I did know. Wren would have died had I not pulled her from that building. And then I would have been just like Theo. Bitter, mean, stupid. All because I missed out on the woman I could have spent forever with.

Knowing what I did now, I couldn't imagine missing this—couldn't imagine losing Wren, losing what we had.

But I had found her, and I had pulled her from those flames, and I mated her, and nothing and no one was going to touch her. Not while I still had breath in my lungs.

I just had to remember that every second of every day, and then that panic that seemed to be camping out in my gut would ease.

Right?

We walked on, weaving through arcaners and tourists alike. So far, nothing had blown up, but that didn't mean that we weren't both on edge. Maybe it was my wolf so restless in my head, maybe it was Wren, or maybe it was real danger, but there was something wrong and I couldn't figure out what it was.

No one was looking at us. Nothing bad had happened. Nothing caught fire or exploded, and I knew there was magic about. So what the fuck was it?

"Nico?" Wren breathed, her hand tightening in mine. "I think we need to head back."

Were we just afraid of the world now? Were we so traumatized that we couldn't imagine even leaving the house anymore?

Wren's fingers tightened on mine, and instead of waiting, she pulled me back down the way we'd come. Everything in me screamed danger, but I could not find the source. Was it everywhere? Was it everything?

The sunshine faded away as storm clouds rolled in, sending a chill up my spine as I moved faster. The wind picked up and so did Wren's steps. Hell, we were practically jogging to get out of The Walk, a sea of tourists and arcaners standing in our way as we threaded through the crowd.

Then the first scent of a Bannister witch reached my nose. It was so different from Wren's jasmine and honey perfume. It was broken promises and lies. It was filth and stench and spent magic. And it filled my senses as if Eloise Bannister herself was right in front of me.

"We have to get out of here," Wren hissed, her grip so tight in mine that my bones rubbed together. "I smell them. My family. They're here."

"I do, too."

"Do you think they'll do something here? Out in the open?" she whispered, her gaze darting everywhere to try and find what we both smelled.

Danger had come calling and I'd been so stupid to have us walk here, so stupid to have her out in the open. I should have protected her better.

Because yes, I did think Wren's family would start some shit out in the open. I did think they would attack us in full view of humans. I believed with everything in me that they would hurt her to try and steal some of her power back.

Lightning flashed in the sky as a rolling crack of thunder shook the earth. Wind whipped through the trees and my wolf was screaming at me to run, to get Wren to safety, to get the fuck out of there before they struck us down.

Gripping Wren's hand tight in mine, I tucked her behind me, bowling through the crowd to the staircase. But more and more people piled onto The Walk, flooding it like they were trying to keep us there. Bodies packed into the crooked narrow lane, swarming us, suffocating us until I felt Wren shove them all back.

Humans squawked in protest at being physically moved, but the arcaners seemed unfazed by the small display of magic. She cleared a path, and we sped up the stairs only to stop dead at the top.

A redheaded woman blocked our way, her palm cracking with an orb of electricity. Humans scattered, screaming, but Wren and I stood stock-still. Dressed in a stained white blouse and wrinkled black slacks, Margot Bannister seemed like she'd seen better days. Her hair was a wild curly mess of snarls and mats, her makeup smeared under her eyes. All the glamour magic she'd done to hide her wrinkles had fizzled and died, aging her face thirty years.

"You did this," she hissed, her gaze locked on

Wren. "You spoiled little brat. We gave you everything, and this is how you repay us?"

It was a struggle to keep Wren behind me because she really wanted to get a piece of her mother.

"You gave me shit. You stole from me. You took what wasn't yours to have and then washed your hands of me. Fuck you, Mother. Your time is over."

The laugh that came out of Margot was hysterical enough to haunt my dreams. "Fuck me? Fuck me? Oh, no, daughter. My time is just beginning. You think I won't take everything you have? You think any of it is yours? You think I won't rip everything from you?"

I didn't wait for the blow that was inevitably coming or for Margot to finish whatever bullshit villain monologue she'd worked herself up for. I just ran.

Dragging Wren behind me, I raced for the house. So many blocks, so far, but Wren could keep up now. She let my hand go and we ran together.

But as fast as we ran, we just weren't fast enough.

CHAPTER SEVENTEEN

NICO

The short trek to our apartment took far too long. Probably because the little more than a mile distance turned into a hike all over the damn city as we attempted to avoid the Bannister clan. It seemed every vehicle was out to hit us, every person on the street came to stand in our way. Shop doors opened to slam into us, and cars jumped curbs to try and mow us down.

Obviously, it was magic, had to be, but that didn't mean it wasn't scary as hell.

"Come on, Wren," a woman cackled. "Come out and play." It wasn't Wren's mother, but it sounded enough like her that it could be an aunt or a cousin maybe?

Not that it mattered who it was exactly. The entire Bannister clan was out in force, ready to steal Wren's power for themselves. The Alpha in me wanted to fight, to stand our ground, but the man in me knew better. Just Wren and I could not go against an entire coven of witches—especially not a coven losing every single bit of sway, clout, and power they'd had for three centuries.

That made them far more dangerous than any pack, any nest, anyone. Because losing power made consequences matter a fuck of a lot less.

Covering Wren with my body, I yanked her out of the way as an orb of electricity sailed past us, detonating against the brick wall. The stone exploded, showering us with shrapnel. Humans yelled, cars honked. It was so loud. My senses were in overdrive, bombarded with everything, but especially the fear—both Wren's and mine.

Honestly, if I didn't know better, I'd think we were getting herded, but I did know better, and I knew this city far better than any Bannister could.

Breathing heavy, I guided us through an alleyway behind Price Hall and around another brand-new brewery I'd already forgotten the name of. Lightning slashed the air overhead as rain pelted us, slowing our steps, making the way more treacherous, but I picked up the pace.

"You can't run, Wren. You can't hide. We'll find you. We'll get what we're owed."

"Judith," Wren whispered, her eyes going wide as a shiver worked its way through her.

Wren had told me about her unhinged aunt who had far too much power harnessed under her skin. My mate's shoulders climbed up to her ears as she pulled ahead of me, running faster, her strides lengthening as she sailed down the street. Like she was drawn to it, she headed straight for home, trying to outrun her family, trying to get under the safety of Fiona's wards.

But the Bannisters seemed to be everywhere. On every corner, in every alley, their magic too much, too powerful, too many.

We needed backup.

Yanking the phone from my pocket, I dialed Wyatt. He was just about the only wolf I still trusted to back me up with no questions asked. He didn't answer, but his voicemail did.

"This is Wyatt. You know what to do."

"I'm sorry for not picking up when you called, but I'm fucked, man," I said on a gasping breath, ducking under an awning as hail pelted the ground around us. "Wren's family is gunning for us, and I need backup." I rattled off the address over the roar of ice smacking the street—just about the only way he'd find the place if he weren't following us. "I'll take all the help I can get, brother."

Meaning, if he wanted to bring my family he could, but I wasn't forcing him to choose me over them. The Acostas had been his only home for so long...

Right before we reached Jones Street, a lightning bolt struck one of the giant oaks, knocking the tree down right in front of us. Cars slammed into the thick trunk, and we crossed the slick road, trying not to get hit.

"Come on," Wren yelled, leading me to a slim alley next to our house. It was only about three feet wide, but it was enough to get us under Fiona's wards and to some backup. I gave her a hand up and followed her over, never so glad in my life that we had a Jacobs witch on our side.

Wren collapsed on the stone pavers, her breaths wheezing in and out of her lungs. "I can't... run... anymore."

She couldn't either. As much as she pulled on my wolf, Wren was losing steam. Her limbs were jelly, her emotions and adrenaline a ball of chaos. We'd have to hole up here and fucking pray the wards held.

But I knew damn well Wren's family were about to give us the fight of our life. I texted Erica, calling for her help as well, but I knew it was a stretch to get the ABI here in time. This was happening now.

"Get inside. Bar the doors."

Wren and I barricaded the glass French doors leading to the courtyard before running up the stairs to Hannah's level. She searched, and I went farther upstairs looking for Fiona and Malia. Both were gone, and by the time I made it back to Wren, I knew Hannah was gone, too.

We were going to have to do this on our own.

Thumps on the roof told me Fiona's wards had shredded like tissue paper, not keeping out a coven of that size. And why would it? The Bannister coven was at least fifty witches deep, and even with waning power, they had enough numbers to rip even the most powerful of wards to shreds.

It was already too late to leave, too late to call anyone, too late to get Wren somewhere safe.

As pissed as I was with my family, we should have gone there. Even if my dad was a bastard, even if he betrayed us, they would have helped us against the Bannisters. I knew that much.

Swallowing hard, I held Wren's hand as we crept back down to our apartment. If the Bannisters knew where we were, we needed stealth to get out of this one.

Stealth and weapons.

In a cabinet under the stairs, I started a small collection with Fiona's help. Potion bombs, handguns, sleeping potions, and enough ammo to start a small war. Usually, I didn't use man-made means to make a kill, but when dealing with witches and as cornered as we were, we'd need it.

"Here," I said, offering Wren her service weapon and a paintball gun filled with sleeping rounds. "And leave off the null wards. We want these to be as effective as they can be."

Wren shivered, but took both guns, fitting the Glock into the belt of her jeans and priming the paintball gun. The echo of a door caving in upstairs rocked through the house, and our eyes met. Wren's were filled with tears she had no intention of shedding, and mine was with the knowledge of what was really about to go down.

Both of us wouldn't make it out of here.

Both of us weren't going to see tomorrow.

Both of us wouldn't stay breathing.

But she would. Wren would live. She would breathe. She would carry on without me.

My gaze tracked to the courtyard. It was still clear. Wren could leave out the back and run while I held them off. She could get to safety. Go to the ABI building where we should have gone in the first fucking place. Erica would protect her.

"I need you to go, Wren," I whispered, staring at those French doors like they were the key to everything. Because I couldn't look at her—not and tell her to leave. "You need to get out of here."

"No." Wren didn't look at me, either. No, she was staring at the door to upstairs like it had done her wrong and she'd really enjoy shooting whoever it was on the other side of it.

Grabbing her shoulder, I made her face me. "I *need* you to go. I can hold them off. You can get safe."

She shrugged me off, planting a hand in my chest. Her fingers fisted in my shirt like she never wanted to let me go. "I'm not going anywhere. You heard me yesterday. The only way I'm leaving is if it's with you. You want to go? Fine. Lead the way. I'll follow you."

Another crash sounded, closer this time. They were on Hannah's level, her aunt's voice calling for Wren with a sing-song tone that had the hairs on the back of my neck standing on end.

We were out of time.

I cupped her face in my hands. "We both aren't going to make it out. I can distract them so you can get somewhere safe. Wren, please. Please, Bird. I need you to be safe."

Wren's tears finally fell, her shuddering breaths heaving in her chest.

"No," she sobbed. "Not without you. I'll never be safe—never be happy—without you. Please just let me stay. I'd rather die by your side than live a thousand years without you in them."

Pressing a fevered kiss to her lips, I prayed there was a way out for us. Because she wasn't going to die in this fucking house at the hands of her family. No way, no how.

Wren's tongue met mine, tasting me like she was saying goodbye.

Like this was our last kiss.

Like the world was ending.

Maybe it was.

When I pulled away, a faint smile touched her lips. A smile that died as magic slammed into the door I was holding shut. The wood splintered, cracked, and Wren's fear flooded our connection. Glass breaking drew my attention, but I'd never been so happy to see who was on the other side of it.

Wyatt shoved through the furniture we used as a barricade, his shoulder landing right next to mine as I struggled to keep the door closed. "You called, boss?"

Nodding, I jerked my head to Wren. "Get her out of here for me, will you? Get her safe. Don't let her out of your sight. You got me?" I swallowed hard, knowing this would be the last time I'd see either of them. "That's an order."

Wyatt straightened, the mirth in his blue eyes dying as he studied my face. He knew exactly what was happening, exactly what I was saying. "Okay, Nic."

Without missing a beat, he latched onto Wren's wrist and tossed her over his shoulder.

"What? No," Wren shouted, kicking and scratching, trying to get out of Wyatt's hold. "Don't do this, Nico. Please."

But Wyatt was fast, so fast Wren didn't have time to get away from him. She didn't have time to say goodbye. But I had all the time in the world to watch her go, her red hair streaming over her teary face—a face that would haunt me in the afterlife.

They sailed up the wall and over it, racing to the safety I could not provide for her.

"I love you, Bird," I whispered, knowing she was far enough away that she couldn't hear me.

The door bulged, the magic on the other side of it shoving me forward.

I'd hold that damn door as long as I could, and

when they killed me, I'd die smiling because I knew Wren was free.

She was free and she was safe, and she was somewhere they wouldn't get her.

But first, I'd take a few of them down with me.

CHAPTER EIGHTEEN

WREN

"Put me down," I ordered, praying I was pulling on just enough of Nico's power that the Alpha would leak out of my voice.

I needed Wyatt to let me go.

I needed him to let me go back.

I needed to get to Nico before my family did.

Please. I'll do anything. I'll pay anything. Just let me keep him safe. Please.

The sound of a car's brakes screeching had Wyatt pausing, his steps faltering enough for me to struggle out of his hold. And yes, I might have kneed him in the stomach on the way down, but that didn't stop him from grabbing my wrist and keeping me from Nico.

"Wren," Ellie yelled from the passenger side of her mother's shit box of a car. "Get in the car. We have to get you out of here."

But I couldn't. I had to go back for Nico. I wasn't hamstrung by that stupid curse they put on me anymore. I could do... *something.* I'd only ever given power away, sure, but I could do something. Anything. I had to try. It was better than just letting him die.

I'd seen the look on my grandmother's face back in Blue Ridge. Even if I wasn't with him, they'd kill Nico out of spite. They'd kill him to hurt me. They'd kill him because they could.

"Get in the car, Wren," Wyatt growled, his wolf so close to the surface, his blue eyes glowed in the low light. The storm was still brewing overhead, ready to rain down from the heavens at any moment. "Don't make me shove you in that gods-damned trunk. Nico wanted you safe, and I'm making that so, even if I have to knock your ass out to do it."

"We don't have much time," Ellie insisted. "Your family is coming, Wren."

Orbs of magic bombarded the house, shaking the very ground we were standing on. My aunt Judith's cackle made all the hairs on my arms stand on end.

She was in there with Nico. She'd do awful things to him. I couldn't leave him.

All of this felt wrong. It felt wrong to leave Nico. It felt wrong to get in a car and speed away. It felt wrong that it was Wyatt here and not my husband. It was wrong that after all we'd survived already that we'd be pulled apart this way.

It wasn't fair.

"I'll fight them. I can do it," I insisted. "Please don't make me leave him."

Wyatt gave me a sympathetic expression as his hands landed on my shoulders, the weight of them too much, too little, too...

"It was his last wish to make you safe. Please let me give him that much."

Tears stung my nose as an ache grew in my chest, in my heart. My gaze fell on the wall that secluded the courtyard.

It was his last wish.

Sobs ripped up my throat as I spun, marching to Ellie's car and opening the door. But as soon as I did, the car itself melted away. Ellie melted away. As if spun by a dream, she dissolved in a puff of smoke.

The door, however, did not, and as much as I tried, I could not let go of it. It transformed before my eyes, morphing from the beat-up tan sedan door with the primer spot into an intricate one made of wood and crystal and vines. It was bigger than I was and nearly three times as wide with an arched top and a rough crystal handle.

Oh. Oh, no. Oh, fuck.

"I don't— What's going on?" I turned to Wyatt, but his face was the picture of regret.

"I didn't want to do this, you know. Sacrificing one for another seemed so wrong. Pen would have hated me for it. But I have to get her back. I have to get my little girl back."

Wyatt's face lost some of its fullness as his skin lightened from the golden tan to a sickly pale. His hair went from a dark blond to a lank brown and he shortened about six inches, his width withering before my eyes.

Wyatt hadn't pulled me from the building.

Wyatt wasn't here.

I didn't know this man, and I didn't know if he was wearing a glamour or—

Pen. Penelope Lewis. An illusion mage missing for twenty-five years.

"Pen is your daughter?" Of all the ways to make a liar out of myself, I chose to go this route. I swore to Nico I wouldn't sacrifice myself for Agent Lewis. I'd sworn I would stay safe, stay with him, and in my one test, I failed.

He nodded. "It was the only way to get her back.

You had to open the door. It had to be your choice."

Of course it had to be my choice. It had been a forced one, but mine, nonetheless. I tried to let go of the crystal handle, but vines from the edges curled around my wrist, making that impossible. Damn if I didn't try, though.

"He swore he'd get her back for me. Swore that she would come home. The Fae have to honor the deals they make."

I didn't have the heart to tell this man that a Fae could twist every single aspect of a deal to suit their needs. He already knew. His eyes said it all. He didn't care if she returned alive or dead, as long as she came back to him.

"Is my family even attacking the house?" I hissed, still trying to yank my hand free as a weight settled in my gut.

Every sleepless night trying not to think about Desmond. Every single nightmare, worrying about the dark Fae out there like the fucking boogeyman, and this asshole just up and made me open the gods-damned Fae door myself. If it weren't so damn smart, I'd start screaming.

The man shook his head. "No. I needed you at this gate in particular. It was the easiest way I could think of to get you here."

My gaze went back to the wall. At least Nico was

safe. No one would hurt him. No one would kill him. I chose not to think about what would befall me, regardless of however long it took to deliver me to Desmond. Or how Nico would feel with me gone. I'd seen his eyes at that damn Italian place. He'd been crazed, panicked.

The illusion bombarding the house died as well, dissolving in a puff of smoke as my aunt Judith's laugh faded away on the wind. The wind itself died, as did the storm, the rain drying up as if it had never been here at all.

I wanted to yell for Nico—I really did—but something made me stop. Yes, he'd be crazed with worry, but he'd be alive. I had no idea what was coming out of that door, and I didn't want Nico to meet that head-on. He'd sacrificed himself to save me.

I'd gladly do the same for him.

So I kept my mouth shut and prayed Nico didn't come out here.

"Do you care that she might not be alive? That he could twist that deal until you end up owing him? You'd sacrifice someone who has never done you wrong for a maybe?"

He tilted his head to the side. "Would you not do the same? I can see inside your head—it's how I create what you most fear. You would sacrifice the world to save your husband. And he would do the same for you. How is it wrong that I would do that for my daughter?"

I couldn't say exactly. Probably because it affected me. Maybe because it hurt Nico, and anyone else who would look for me.

But before I could say any of that, a dark-haired man dressed all in black strode from the open door.

"Where is she?" the illusion mage demanded, a long sword forming in his hand.

"Your tricks don't work on me, mage, just like your daughter's never worked on my father."

The mage ground his teeth, straightening like he knew something the man in black did not. "Do you know what illusion mages can do when they get to be my age? They make dream reality. Don't test me. Where is Penelope? Where is my daughter?"

The man in black firmed his mouth, raising a single eyebrow as he gestured to the open door. Two people walked out of it. One was a lanky man with a hunched back and ripped clothes, and the other was a woman who looked no older than I did. She struggled with her cane, favoring the wrong side of it like she'd never used one before. And that was likely due to the prosthetic she was using, which appeared to be made of a living wood carved into the shape of a foot.

"Penelope," he breathed, reaching for the woman and snatching her off her feet, his sword gone in a puff of smoke.

"Papa?"

And while this was touching and all, I was still trying to get the fucking door to let me go. Because I knew damn well what happened after this. If the deal was complete, then I was the price paid, and I had no intention of going through that damn door.

Force wasn't working, so I tried a little magic, shoving power into the vines in the hopes that it shocked them somehow. But shoving power into them only tightened them on my skin, the damn things growing stronger.

Perfect.

"I suggest you make your way, mage," the man in black advised, tucking his hair behind a very pointed ear. "The wolf will follow your scent soon enough."

The mage nodded, tucking his daughter under his arm and disappearing into another puff of fucking smoke. If I made it out of this, I would wrap a null ward around his neck and kick him in the junk.

Then the Fae's gaze moved to me. "And you. For someone so powerful, you seem to fuck up a whole lot. Who falls for an illusion mage's tricks?"

With nothing else for it, I flipped the asshole off.

"People who can't see through them, dipshit. Got any more probing questions?"

A faint smile tipped up his lips. "My father is going to hate you. Personally, I love it. His plaything is a mouthy youngling with magic she can't control. It serves him right."

Oh, goodie, just what I always wanted. To be a plaything for a fucking tyrant.

"You seem to dislike dear old dad. Why don't you make this door let me go and I'll skip off into the sunset. No muss, no fuss."

Was I trying to strike a Fae deal? Had I sniffed glue in the last thirty seconds, and no one told me?

"You see, I would. You seem nice enough. A little rough around the edges, but nothing too bad. You don't deserve what's about to happen. But I need him occupied and contained while I seal these bloody doors shut, and you're just the proper distraction. Sorry, love, them's the breaks."

He lifted his chin to the squirrely looking dude who I could break in half with a good poke to the ribs. "I'll see to it your family is taken care of."

"Wait," I pleaded, realizing a little late what was going on. "Don't do this. I have to get out. I have to get the rest of them out." Because if Penelope was alive after twenty-five years, the other women could be, too. I'd sort of made peace with the fact that I was going in there. I hadn't with the fact that I might not come back out.

Dark eyes speared me with regret. "There is no getting out. Not for you, Wren Bannister, and not for anyone else left in the Fae realm. We've done enough damage. It's time for these doors to die."

The skinny guy wrapped his spindly hand around my bicep, his grip far stronger than I'd thought it was going to be. "Come on, witch."

At his words, the vines unwrapped from my wrist, and I was free—or rather free-ish. I tried yanking my arm from his grip, but I couldn't move him an inch.

"Let me go," I screeched, planting my feet as he tried pulling me toward the door.

"Wren," Nico shouted, his voice so welcome and so not all at the same time. I met his gaze, finding it instantly as if my eyes were drawn to him. He was coming over the wall, somehow knowing exactly where I was. In an instant, Nico jumped to his wolf, the animal racing for us, trying to get to me before I was dragged into oblivion.

The Fae in black sighed as he shot darkness from his hand, the oily blackness so thick it was like a wall separating Nico from the rest of us.

"I am sorry for this, Wren. Maybe one day you'll

understand why I had to do this. Maybe you'll know it was the right decision."

But I wasn't listening to the Fae. I was still trying to rip my arm from the iron grip of the spindly man and get to my mate.

"Nico," I pleaded, but before I could get away, I was through the door, and it was closing on us. "Nico!"

The door sealed shut, cutting off all light, all warmth. The air in this blackness was cold, cold and wet and smelled of death. And I wanted no part of going wherever this dude wanted me to.

"Let me go," I yelled, my voice echoing off what sounded like stone.

Instantly, the man let me go. "If that's what you want," he said as I stumbled and fell, landing hard on my ass on the rough, cold ground. "But I can see in the dark. Can you?"

A few days ago, I could, but... That was with me drawing on Nico's wolf. That was with a shifter's eyes, a shifter's power. I had a feeling that as far away as Nico was, there was no way I could use what he'd given me. Now, I was stuck with what I'd been born with and that wasn't the greatest night vision.

"No, I can't," I admitted, slowly getting to my feet. After having Nico's wolf for just a few days, the lack of light and sound and smell made me feel like my head was under water.

"Then, I'll guide you," he said, latching onto my hand. "Try not to talk to Desmond too much. He'll twist your words until you've agreed to something you had no intention of agreeing to. That's how Pen lost her foot."

No talking. Got it.

"My name is Cyrus, by the way, and we are sorry for this. Tristan never wanted to entrap you, but it was the only way. He couldn't take another woman being sold—another life wasted. I'll try to keep you out of the thick of it."

Those were the last words Cyrus spoke for a very long while. We walked down that dark corridor for what seemed like hours, our steps echoing off the stone enough to rattle my brain.

And by the time we made it to anything resembling light, I began to wish I would have stayed in that damned hallway forever.

CHAPTER NINETEEN

WREN

The light in the Fae realm was a dim, weak illumination from a muted sun and too much hazy cloud cover. The large windows of the throne room—or what I assumed was a throne room—let what passed for sunshine through, painting the scene of what I figured Hell might look like if it were trying too hard.

The floors were blood-red and black—either from actual blood or a design choice from some macabre stylist's nightmare. The walls seemed to bleed a dark-red sap that could have been actual blood or something else entirely. The throne itself was black, high-backed, and tufted with a material that could have been velvet or something more sinister like skin or hair. Cages were suspended from the ceiling, some all the way up to impossible heights and some almost touching the floor. Each of them held a person or an animal, each of them smelled like literal death, and each one ticked my anger up about a zillion notches.

It was incredibly difficult to be scared when I wanted to commit murder.

The man on the throne seemed bored, like a spoiled child looking for his next plaything. But that wasn't to say he wasn't beautiful. Just like his son, Desmond was dark-haired and dressed in all black. His jaw was sharp, his cheekbones prominent, and his lips full. His hair fell in a sleek waterfall, only interrupted by what might be a bone crown filled with sparkling stones. But where his son's eyes were a rich brown, Desmond's were the palest blue, the irises glowing in the low light like glittering diamonds.

He sat casually, one ankle resting on the other knee but exuded a manic sort of calm, as if everything from his posture to his crown was fake. As if everything I saw was affected rather than natural. Even the foliage outside was a pale representation of spooky trees, their limbs like fingers reaching to the sky.

Honestly, I was having trouble not rolling my eyes.

Okay, sure, in theory all this was scary. Of course in a normal person's brain, bleeding walls and prisoners strung up in cages would be the height of fear. But at a certain point, it was like, "Okay, we get it already." It reminded me of those haunted houses Ellie and I used to go to when we were teenagers that were so over the top, they were hilarious. This whole thing—from the realm to the king to the castle itself —was just trying too hard.

Cyrus let go of my hand as we approached the raised platform, moving ahead of me as if to announce the fact that we were here. Fair enough.

"Sire, I have procured Wren Bannister as requested," Cyrus said, bowing so low it was a wonder he didn't melt into the floor.

Desmond's smile could have been alluring if it wasn't so joyless. His eyes were dead, the upturn to his lips fake, his whole posture just...

This was the man I'd been too scared to think about?

This was the guy I was supposed to be afraid of?

He was a fucking joke.

And procured? Was that a fancy way of saying he kidnapped me and dragged my ass down here? Because the euphemism was lacking.

"Very good, Cyrus," Desmond said on a sigh, but not one of pleasure. It was as if he was bored with himself, too. "You may leave us. Take your pet Elizabeth with you as a reward."

Cyrus shot me a repentant expression before opening the cage closest to my left. From it, he lifted a small woman from the confines and cradled her to his chest. Cyrus had said he'd try to help me, but he was more worried about the woman in his arms than me at the moment.

I couldn't say I blamed him. And I wasn't sure I needed his help, anyway.

"Well, on with it," Desmond ordered, peeling something rancid from the wooden platter to his right and slurping it into his mouth. "Show me your power."

Frowning, I just stood there. Unless he planned on using magic of his own, I was sort of at a loss. I knew I had power, but using it? Well, that was the rub, wasn't it?

"Do you speak, girl? Or are you a mute?"

Tilting my head to the side, I examined the dark Fae. I should have really saved all my worry for my family. Aunt Judith had this guy beat on her worst day and Eloise? Eloise would eat him for breakfast and shit him out by lunch. Hell, even the illusion mage's nightmare was scarier than this.

"Desmond, I take it. Hmm." I hummed my disapproval just like old Eloise would. Normally, I would hate the lessons my grandmother had taught me, but ripping someone's psyche apart with just my tone and words was a skill I'd picked up from her. And damn if I wasn't taught by a fucking master. "I thought you'd be taller."

If there is one thing I excelled at, it was annoying the fuck out of people—*just ask Grandma*. Might as well figure out where this asshole's buttons were, and the only way to do that was by pressing all of them. At once.

"And cuter." I tapped on my bottom lip, letting my gaze roam his body. He enjoyed imprisoning people? He enjoyed making people suffer? Well, he was going to know what it was like to be treated like a thing. "I suppose movies really have surpassed reality—even Fae reality. Pity."

Desmond's eyes flashed a darker blue as his smile faded. His relaxed posture tightened as he sat up straighter, his feet finding the floor.

"You would do well to watch your tongue before I cut it from your head."

First blood. A complete poser and vain to boot? Oh, this was going to be sweet.

"Big talk from a guy who had to send a runner to

fetch me. Did I hurt your feelings?" I faked a pout. "Do you need a hug?"

If I was going to be here a while—and I sort of figured I would be, considering Desmond's son planned on closing the Fae gates forever and all—then I wanted to make this guy's life a living fucking hell. If everyone and everything I loved was lost to me? Well, he was going to really regret asking me to talk.

"I mean this is a hell of a lot of posturing you've got going on here," I said, gesturing to well, everything. "This is the Unseelie Court and not Hell, right? I mean, I'm not hating the whole torture and pain thing you've got going on, I just think you might need a little help with the execution is all. It has the air of trying too hard, don't you think? Plus, you might need to fire your decorator. Pronto."

Desmond leaned forward in his chair, practically vibrating with rage. *Oh, touchy, touchy.* Maybe he was the designer here.

"Maybe I'll cut out your eyes since you hate the place so much. See how you like it in the dark."

My smile had to be simpering, but that was what I was going for. "Just jumping in with all the clichés right off the bat, huh? Not going to space them out, or anything? Talk about blowing your wad too early."

Desmond flew from his chair, a blade in hand,

seemingly conjured from nothing. He was on me before I could even blink. But even as I felt the breeze of the knife slide through me, the pain never came.

Opening both my eyes, I stared in shock as the cold weight in my middle seemed to intensify just a smidge. And that was because Desmond's hand—knife and all—was indeed in the general vicinity of my stomach. The problem for him was the blade, hand, and the wrist attached to it all sort of just passed on through.

Like I was a ghost or an apparition or... I didn't know what. What I did know was that Desmond seemed rather put out that his blade did exactly fuck all. He moved to backhand me, but his hand slid through my head like I was made of smoke.

I had no idea what was going on. I had definitely been hit before. Girard had done it not even a week ago, and I distinctly remembered Diana's knife slicing through my throat. That didn't mean I wasn't going to run with it, though.

"Wow. This must be really embarrassing for you. Big, bad dark Fae and you can't even hurt me. I've heard impotency is a real self-esteem killer." I sucked in a breath through my teeth as I let my gaze drift in the direction of his crotch. "Ouch."

Desmond reached for my face, his fingertips passing through my flesh. "What are you?"

Shrugging, I skirted around the arguably tall Fae, wondering if I could touch things or if things just couldn't touch me.

"I don't know. I suppose you could call me a witch, but that's not quite right, now, is it? Your guess is as good as mine. You're the one who wanted me here. You tell me, Tinkerbell."

Stopping at the first cage I could reach, I swept my hand over the lock. If I could touch it, I could pick it—in theory. If I could pick it, then I could get these people out of here. Again, in theory. Who knew if Tristan was successful in closing the Fae portals?

Who knew if Nico had broken through his magic and ripped him limb from limb?

One could only hope.

The cold stone-like metal brushed against my skin without passing through, the first win of the day. But it still didn't tell me why I could touch things, but Desmond couldn't touch me—a fact that became clearer and clearer since his Fae ass was currently trying to punch me in the head.

"This must be a huge bummer, right. I mean first you try to nab me yourself, but that backfires," I said, ticking off his failures on my fingers, completely ignoring his attempts to hurt me. "Then you try to get Girard to do it, but he shits the bed—not once, but three times. Now your son handles your little fuck-up, but you can't touch me. Which Fate did you piss off, buddy?"

Yeah, I was getting out of here, and I was taking every single prisoner with me. I just needed a plan that did not involve me stumbling around in the dark like an idiot.

"The Fates have no dominion here," he growled, his body right in my bubble.

My smile was simpering as I let my gaze travel down his body and up to his face. "Clearly. If they did, maybe they'd hire you a decent decorator."

I turned my back to him, exploring the throne room. Based on the coppery smell, it was indeed blood running down the walls, but I wasn't sure if it was arcaner blood, Fae blood, or some kind of animal. The throne was also made of burned skin? And his crown—which I hadn't gotten a good look at before—was made from bones and pretty blue jewels that matched his eyes.

Again, the try-hard in this place was fucking pathetic, and I was already bored. I needed to get back to Nico before he lost his mind, and this whole thing was getting in the way of that.

"Well, hoss, I'm assuming you wanted me here for a reason, and I doubt it's to listen to the tale of how your supplier of arcaner playthings got his throat ripped out. So what is it? Why go to all this trouble?" I gave him my most pitying expression. "Were you bored? You look bored. Fuck, I'm bored, and I just got here."

That was it, wasn't it? I wasn't scared here because I had nothing to lose. Everything I wanted was back home. Every threat? It was far away where he couldn't reach. My happiness? Was with Nico, with my friends, with the small little family I made for myself.

And I wanted it back.

"You are supposed to be an amplifier, a way to tap into all the power I have been denied. You're supposed to bring me my throne," he hissed, wanting to smack me around but missing the mark over and over again.

My whole body pivoted to the skin chair and back. "You mean that tacky thing? Weren't you just sitting on it?"

Desmond skirted around me, heading for the chair. "Stupid girl. This is not my realm and not my throne. This is my prison and yours. The Seelie Queen stuck me here when our marriage deteriorated, the petty bitch."

"Of course, and I'm sure nothing at all predicated said alienation. You're clearly the saint in this whole situation."

Yes, and I was a purple alien named Blerp.

"You will hold your tongue, witch," he said, his voice taking on a sort of influence, kind of like when Nico did his Alpha thing, but far less effective.

"Sorry." I shrugged. "That's not really my style. Can I offer you a sarcastic comment?"

Desmond's eyes narrowed and he stroked his chin like a gods-damned vaudeville villain. "I can't touch you. I can't influence you. But I wonder if my other pets can. I've collected many pretty pets over the years, you know."

A tiny little trickle of fear threaded through the boredom. Cyrus could touch me, and if Cyrus could, it was completely possible Desmond's other prisoners could, too. And I really hoped the *what the fuck* I was thinking wasn't showing on my face.

Because the illusionist had been very thorough in his conjuring, and that gun I had stuffed into my belt? Well, it was nothing more than air. The paintball gun filled with sleeping potion? Never existed. The potion bombs I'd stuffed in my pocket?

Yep. You guessed it. Gone just like all his other delusions in a puff of fucking smoke.

That didn't mean I didn't have any weapons at my disposal. There were chains and rocks and...

Okay, unless I found a sword somewhere or a really fancy handgun, I was fucked.

And this is why we keep our mouths shut, Wren. So we don't anger Fae Kings into getting creative with their punishments.

"If that's what you want, hoss. But how is that getting you your throne again? I thought you wanted power. Power I seem to have and you don't. Personally, I think you're going about this all wrong —especially since all the power in the world isn't going to help you get out of here."

I was totally bullshitting, but throwing Desmond's son under the bus was about the only card I had.

"Because your son closed down the Fae gates all nice and tight. I have a feeling you can't open them, either. He sent me here as a distraction, and just like a toddler with a brand-new toy, you fell right for it."

Desmond let out a little whistle, snapping his fingers as a real smile finally stretched across his face.

I didn't see the rock aimed for my temple until it was too late, but I sure as shit felt it. Light bloomed in my skull as the pain slammed into me.

And the last thing I saw was Desmond tossing his head back and laughing like a villain in a cartoon.

Prick.

CHAPTER TWENTY

WREN

I was getting really tired of concussions. Like, was it me? Was I a head injury magnet of some kind? Or was I just usually in the wrong place at the wrong time with the wrong powers and a big fucking mouth.

Groaning, I tried peeling myself from the cold floor. After doing this once already this month, I remembered to sit up slowly and hope for no vomiting. The stench from the place was atrocious, so the "no vomiting" thing was tenuous at best, but I did what I could.

My cell was made of stone and a living sort of metal. And by living, the shit seemed to breathe, the cracks lit by an ominous green glow that brightened and dimmed with each breeze that flit through the space.

Cozy.

Other than a bucket and a set of bars, the cell was barren, the light only from the bars themselves and the torch sconces dotting the corridor beyond. Moans echoed through the dungeon—and this was most definitely a dungeon—like I was stuck on a haunted house playlist on repeat.

"Of all the places you could have found yourself in, you made it all the way down here," a woman scolded, scaring the absolute shit out of me. My head whipped to the left and right, but no one—and I did mean no one—was there.

A moment later, a woman appeared at my bars, a golden light in the middle of this darkness as she surveyed my predicament. Her hair was the darkest of blacks while her skin was a warm bronze that reminded me of sunshine and springtime and long, lazy days by the pool. Sharp eyebrows and cheekbones were tempered by a dusting of freckles across her nose and her eyes resembled the greenest of grasses.

"Yes, because getting kidnapped is the height of fun for me," I muttered, trying to peel my ass off the floor. So far, I'd only managed my upper body, but I'd get there. Eventually. *"What do you want to do today, Wren? Get kidnapped? Sounds swell.* Circumstances are out of my control. Obviously."

Her face—as pretty as it was—got infinitely less pretty when she gave me a skeptical glance. "Who falls for an illusionist's magic? Not once, but enough they don't even think to bring a weapon—"

Okay, that was it. "Not all of us can see through them, you know. And I appreciate the visit and all, but who are you, and why are you interrupting my perfectly good nap with insults and *judgeyness*?"

The lady fit a hand to her hip. "You were much more pleasant as a toddler. I remember you distinctly saying I was the most beautiful woman you'd ever seen."

That... was new information. "Still true, but that doesn't tell me who you are."

"Call me Áine. To others I'm known as the Seelie Queen. To my ex-husband I'm the definition of Hell itself. Really, it depends on who you ask."

"And we've met before?"

She leaned closer. "You caught that, did you? I wondered, with the head injury and all. I suppose I'll have to fill you in now that Eloise has wiped me from your brain." She studied my face like I was particularly interesting.

Then a tremor shook through the place, the

torches flared as the bar began to glow brighter. "Quick and dirty version, then?"

"Uh... sure?"

She smiled as if she was remembering a fond memory. "At four years old, you went on an adventure during... I believe a field trip with your school. Instead of the safe outing to a park with small children, it turned into you falling through a Fae door right into my throne room."

That... was not the story I got, and trying to think about it made my head hurt. I rubbed my temple, suppressing a gag when the world shook again.

"You walked right up to me and called me beautiful and asked for me to take you home. But when I tried to touch you, to take your hand, it passed right through."

"Sounds familiar," I groaned, the spike in my head doubling in strength.

The ground shook a little more, harder this time, and it took everything in me to not vomit all over the floor.

"Yes, well, we might not be able to touch you, but you, my dear, can touch us. You grabbed my hand and ordered me to take you home. That your mother would be worried. And so, I did."

I tried remembering anything about this but all I got was one big blank.

"You'd been gone so long, people had stopped looking for you. But I still honored the promise I made and brought you to your mother. I had no idea when I did, or just what they'd do to you, or how much power they would steal. Honestly, I am a much better judge of character."

"This is an awesome story of my childhood that I had no idea existed and all, but mind telling me why the earth is shaking like a damn maraca?"

"Okay, I see it now. You were just as precocious as a child." She studied me a little longer. "The reason the earth is shaking is because you are not supposed to be here. And the sooner I get you home, the better. But first, you need to get yourself out of that cell."

The world rattled again, harder this time, nearly knocking me off my feet. "Love to, lady. You got a manual in your pocket on how to do that or…"

"I really ought to turn your grandmother into a slug or something. She taught you nothing? After all the instruction I gave her? Honestly." Áine rolled her eyes and fit both hands on her hips. "You can give power, sure, but you can take it as well. Not just from others, but from the very universe itself. You draw on the energy of the ether no matter where you are. As a child born under particularly auspicious stars, it is all at your disposal. It is up to you to use it."

Super. That just cleared everything right up.

"If I wanted to open a door in a place like this, I might draw on the magic that held the door shut. Rendering it inert."

Maybe it was the head injury, maybe it was the pretty lady in the gold gown, but I figured it couldn't hurt to try. A careful step later, and I was hanging onto the bars for dear life as the world rocked again. This time, the stone ceiling cracked, hissing like a snake as it settled.

Okay, it was time to move this shit along. But I'd only ever given magic, I didn't know how to take it.

"Remember the feeling of Nico healing you, taking away your pain, siphoning it into himself. Try it that way."

Swallowing hard, I did what she said, trying to pull the magic into myself like Nico would have done to my wounds. This magic was dark, not putrid, but not good, either. It was almost a living, breathing thing, and it hissed in pain as I took from it. But the light in the bars died, the lock clanking open with a welcome thud.

"Very good. Now let's get out of here." Áine held out her hand.

I didn't take it—too wary of too much help. Especially in this place. "Lead the way."

Smiling, she turned, leading me down the hallway at a fast clip I could barely keep up with.

And I followed her until I got to the next cell. The smell was awful, but the girl on the ground was barely older than I was. Dressed in tattered rags, she was curled in on herself, shivering.

"Wait. Can't we bring them?" I grabbed onto her bars, pulling with the same sort of energy I'd used on my own.

"Stop," Áine hissed as another tremor rocked the entire foundation to its core. "We don't have time. This world is eating itself with you here. We have to go. Now. If we don't, there will be nothing and no one left for you to save." She reached for me again, her palm upturned. "Take my hand, Wren. I'll bring you back—to your world, to your Nico. That's what you want, isn't it?"

Shaking my head, I dropped my hold on the bars. "Prove you can't touch me, and I'll follow you."

Maybe it was my general distrust of literally anything in this place, but I didn't think taking Áine's hand was such a good idea. Sighing, she placated me, her fingers passing through my body like vapor.

"See. No Fae can harm you here. Please. I just want to take you home before this world implodes and takes mine with it."

She forcefully shook her hand in front of my face, begging me to take the offered help. "Fine. But if shit goes sideways, I'm coming back here and watching this place turn to dust myself."

Áine huffed out a laugh. "I would expect nothing less."

Reluctantly, I put my hand in hers, and as soon as I did, we didn't just move. We moved. A moment later, we weren't in that dungeon anymore, we were at the base of a mountain, its dark spires reaching for the muted sky.

Áine gestured to a door, the crystal handle and vined detail very familiar. "My son closed many doors, but not all of them. This will take you back to your world, but you need to hurry. I fear once again, you've been gone too long."

Warily, I grabbed the handle, turning the crystal in my palm as the world shook again. A fissure opened up in between Áine and I, the earth falling away as I threw the door open and jumped inside.

"Be careful, young Wren. And hurry," Áine called and then the door shut, sealing me in the same darkness that had enveloped me on the way here.

Shakily, I stood, running my fingers against the cool stone walls, pressing forward in the dark. I walked for what felt like hours, the tunnel getting warmer as I trudged home, hoping the next turn, the next step was the one to take me back.

After a while I got scared, a feeling I hadn't quite

had in the Fae realm. Was it because it felt fake? Was it the realm itself that leeched my fear? Or was it too close to a childhood memory of getting shoved into a closet for my liking?

A question for the ages.

Faintly up ahead, an orange glow filtered into the hall, softly illuminating the rough bricks and unlit sconces. I couldn't help it, I raced for the light, praying this was it, this was home, this was...

The door itself was hot to the touch, almost burning, and if I hadn't been trapped in the fucking dark, I would have thought about what that might mean before I shoved it open. Fire raged beyond, consuming a large oak tree like it was dry kindling. The grass was burning embers and the roar of it all filled my ears.

But I couldn't go back, I could only go forward.

Stomach churning, I headed for the lone spot that seemed safe, a small patch of green in a sea of flames. My skin scalded as I ran, the smoke burning my lungs as I raced through the blaze. Shaking, I landed on the lone patch of green earth before scrambling farther into the street. A fire engine screamed down the road, nearly taking me out as I crossed to safety.

It took me a second to get my bearings. This was the earth realm, and this was Savannah, but the place was in chaos. People walked right by like there wasn't a huge blaze just taking out Chatham Square. Cars screeched as people crossed the street without warning. And no one seemed too concerned about the flames jumping from tree to tree or that they might take out the houses next.

Home. I needed to go home. Orienting myself, I headed north, cutting through an alley to the courtyard. Only, when I struggled over the wall, nothing seemed right. All the ivy was dead, and the house was dark. That ivy had been lush and green just hours ago. The French doors leading to my apartment were shattered to bits, hanging from the hinges in pieces. My apartment was empty, dust covered everything, my stuff gone.

"Nico," I yelled, the fear really coming in strong now. "I'm home."

But the house echoed with my calls. I raced up the stairs, the stale air hitting my nose as I forced open the door to Hannah's level. Dried blood smeared the hallway hardwood leading to the front door, and the alarm bells just would not stop ringing in my head.

"Fiona? Malia? Hannah? Nico? Somebody answer me."

But all I got was silence. Silence when I checked every room, every closet. Silence when I picked up the house phone, only to get nothing but static. Silence when I cried at the bottom of the steps, the fear clawing up my throat.

Was I dead? Did I die? Did they?

Swallowing hard, I pulled myself up. Someone had to have answers. Someone had to be breathing. Someone had to know something.

The only other place I could think of to go was the same place I'd gone when I'd skinned my knee as a kid and where I'd gone when I'd gotten stood up freshman year.

Ellie and Alice.

But the Savannah I'd left was not the same one I'd come back to. Stores were boarded up and restaurants closed. The streetlights were off or broken and the traffic ones were blinking red in all directions. Trash burned in barrels in the alley, even though it was sticky hot outside and the people surrounding them held their hands out for warmth.

I picked up the pace, running the last two miles to Ellie's as if someone or something was following me.

Ellie's house was different, too. The windows had bars on them, for one, and two? There were cameras pointed in every direction. Salt covered the entirety of her stoop, the granules crunching underfoot as I banged on the screen door.

"Ellie," I called, practically shivering in fear.

She had to be home. Had to be. She was home and alive and so was I and things were fine. They were fine.

Far too many moments later, the door opened, a double-barreled shotgun leading the way with Ellie right behind it. I backed up a step, tossing my hands in the air as I got off her front porch.

"Ellie?"

"Wren?" she breathed, her eyes wide as saucers. Shakily, she unloaded the shotgun and unchained the bars, wrapping her arms around me in a hug so tight it healed a part of my soul.

I was alive. I was really here, and I wasn't dead in the Fae realm somewhere. I made it.

"Where have you been? It's been so long. We all thought you were dead." She rocked back and forth, not letting me go for an instant.

"I don't understand. What happened? I was gone for a day—tops—and I come back and it's like *Mad Max* and the fucking *Thunderdome*. What is going on? Where is everyone? Where is Nico and Alice and my friends?"

Ellie pulled away and met my gaze, gripping my shoulders like she'd fall down if she let me go.

"What do you mean you were gone for a day?" She shook her head like she was trying to make it make sense. "Do you think all this happened in a single day?"

By the look on my face, she seemed to realize a very bad thing, something that I was beginning to arrive at myself.

"It hasn't been a day, has it?"

Ellie shook her head again, her grip getting stronger as my legs threatened to give out.

"It's been three years, Wren. The Savannah you knew—the life you knew? It's gone."

Bile churned in my belly. Three years? Three?

"And Nico? Where is he?"

Tears filled Ellie's eyes as she held me up. "I don't know."

Heat flashed over my skin, like I was right back in those flames. Ellie might not know where Nico was, but I would. I'd find him.

Even if I had to burn the rest of this city down to do it.

Thank you so much for reading Magic & Mayhem. I can't express just how much I love Wren & Nico and their ragtag bunch of friends. And we aren't quite done yet!

Next up is Errors & Exorcisms and all the crazy, witchy shenanigans that is to come. I hope

you're buckled in to see Wren & Nico contend with the three years Wren missed, the Fae Realm... oh, and their crazy mate bond!

GET IT NOW!

Want the skinny on future releases without having to follow me absolutely everywhere on social media?
Text "LEGION" to (844) 311-5791

ERRORS & EXORCISMS

The Wrong Witch Book Three

Savannah is a Hell of a city...

After a quick jaunt to the Fae realm, I've come home
to find my city on fire, my mate nowhere to be found,
and demons running in the streets. Now, I have to
help close a portal to Hell while also trying to figure
out why my wonky powers are destroying reality as I
know it.

And I will. Right after I find my wolf...

Get it now!

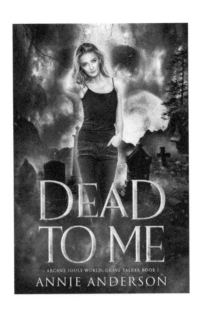

Want more in the Arcane Souls World?
Check out...

DEAD TO ME
Grave Talker Book One

Meet Darby. Coffee addict. Homicide detective.
Oh, and she can see ghosts, too.

There are only three rules in Darby Adler's life.
One: Don't talk to the dead in front of the living.
Two: Stay off the Arcane Bureau of Investigation's radar.
Three: Don't forget rules one and two.

With a murderer desperate for Darby's attention and an ABI agent in town, things are about to get mighty interesting in Haunted Peak, TN.

Grab Dead to Me today!

Want more in the Arcane Souls World?
Check out...

NIGHT WATCH
Soul Reader Book One

Waking up at the foot of your own grave is no picnic... especially when you can't remember how you got there.

There are only two things Sloane knows for certain: how to kill bad guys, and that something awful turned her into a monster. With a price on her head and nowhere to run, choosing between a job and a bed or certain death sort of seems like a no-brainer.

If only there wasn't that silly rule about not killing people...

Grab Night Watch today!

THE ROGUE ETHEREAL SERIES

an adult urban fantasy series by Annie Anderson

Enjoy the The Wrong Witch Series?
Then you'll love Max!

Come meet Max. She's brash. She's inked. She has a
bad habit of dying... *a lot.* She's also a Rogue with a
demon on her tail and not much backup.
This witch has a serious bone to pick.

Check out the Rogue Ethereal Series today!

THE PHOENIX RISING SERIES

an adult paranormal romance series by Annie Anderson

Heaven, Hell, and everything in between. Fall into the realm of Phoenixes and Wraiths who guard the gates of the beyond. That is, if they can survive that long...

Living forever isn't all it's cracked up to be.

Check out the Phoenix Rising Series today!

EXCLUSIVE SNEAK PEEKS,
GIVEAWAYS, BOOK DISCUSSION.
COME FOR THE BOOKS.
STAY FOR THE MEMES.

To stay up to date on all things Annie Anderson, get exclusive access to ARCs and giveaways, and be a member of a fun, positive, drama-free space, join The Legion!

ACKNOWLEDGMENTS

A huge, honking thank you to Shawn, Barb, Jade, Angela, Heather, Kelly, and Erin. Thanks for the late-night calls, the endurance of my whining, the incessant plotting sessions, the wine runs, the trauma I put you through...

Basically, thanks for putting up with my bullshit.

Every single one of you rock and I couldn't have done it without you.

ABOUT THE AUTHOR

 Annie Anderson is the author of the international bestselling Rogue Ethereal series. A United States Air Force veteran, Annie pens fast-paced Urban Fantasy novels filled with strong, snarky heroines and a boatload of magic. When she takes a break from writing, she can be found binge-watching The Magicians, flirting with her husband, wrangling children, or bribing her cantankerous dogs to go on a walk.

To find out more about Annie and her books, visit
www.annieande.com

facebook.com/AuthorAnnieAnderson

twitter.com/AnnieAnde

instagram.com/AnnieAnde

amazon.com/author/annieande

bookbub.com/authors/annie-anderson

goodreads.com/AnnieAnde

pinterest.com/annieande

tiktok.com/@authorannieanderson